She was more beautiful than he remembered, the delicate, perfectly formed body still unbelievably sexy.

Five years ago he could have taken that body; it had been his for the asking. He narrowed his eyes, black gleaming through the enigmatic, heavy sweep of his lashes.

Now, one way or another, he was going to have her. Take what he wanted for as long as he wanted it, learn the secrets of her delectable body, then toss her back where she belonged.

Dropping his hands, he leaned farther back in the chair. His accent slightly more pronounced than usual, his tone smooth as cream, he said, "I have a proposition to put to you, Miss Pennington…."

RED HOT REVENGE

Diana Hamilton

A SPANISH VENGEANCE

RED HOT REVENGE

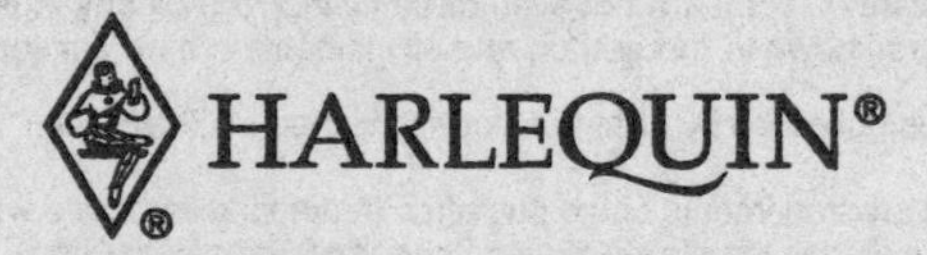

TORONTO • NEW YORK • LONDON
AMSTERDAM • PARIS • SYDNEY • HAMBURG
STOCKHOLM • ATHENS • TOKYO • MILAN • MADRID
PRAGUE • WARSAW • BUDAPEST • AUCKLAND

ISBN 0-373-12368-X

A SPANISH VENGEANCE

First North American Publication 2004.

This edition published by arrangement with Harlequin Books S.A.

Visit us at www.eHarlequin.com

Printed in U.S.A.

CHAPTER ONE

A *DEEPLY* unsettling mixture of frazzled nerve ends and sizzling excitement was making Lisa Pennington feel decidedly queasy.

Long fingers fumbled in her envelope purse, searching for a tissue to mop the perspiration from her face. She was sweating like a foundry worker. She tried to convince herself it was down to the heat of the Spanish evening sun and told herself to snap out of it. She'd end up looking a real soggy mess if she didn't pull herself together. And that mustn't happen.

She had to look good, cool and calm, if only to counteract Ben's reaction. So she'd pulled out all the stops, and dug out her make-up bag. The creamy foundation toned down the tan she'd acquired during the last eight weeks, while silvery eye-shadow emphasised the size and shape of her inky-blue eyes, and scarlet lipstick gave her the illusion of courage.

She'd slopped around in shorts and cool cotton tops all through this holiday but this evening she was wearing a dress in silvery-green silk, sleek and hopefully sophisticated. She couldn't be seen in the newest, smartest hotel in the whole of Marbella wearing any old rag.

Tomorrow she, Ben and Sophie would be returning to England. By tomorrow everyone would know what

Diego's intentions were. She quivered, assailed by a fresh onslaught of nervous tension.

Diego. Oh, how she loved him—she couldn't describe how much! In the last seven weeks he had become her whole world, the focus of every thought, of every breath she drew. And he loved her; she knew he did. The knowledge was pure magic. Tonight he would make his intentions plain. Why else would he have suggested he meet with her and her holiday companions in the disco bar of the exclusive hotel? He knew how close Ben and Sophie were to her, twin offspring of her father's business partner. The three of them had always been mates, especially after the death of her mother four years ago when they had taken her under their loving, protective wings.

Lisa crossed her fingers, praying that the coming meeting would go smoothly, that Ben wouldn't come out with something Diego's Spanish pride would never let him forgive. It would be unbearable if the three people she loved best in the world were at daggers drawn.

Straightening her shoulders, feeling the long silky fall of her silver-blonde hair brush against the bare skin of her back, she risked a sideways glance. Ben, strolling at her side, was seemingly intent on watching the expensive cars cruising the elegant sea front. He wasn't looking at her but she knew his bluntly good looking features would be clenched with displeasure if he did turn in her direction.

At twenty years of age he was only two years her senior yet he sometimes acted as if he were her grandfather! Lisa sighed, remembering his stinging comments when, in order to explain why she'd spent little time with him and Sophie, she'd had to confess that she'd met someone.

Flushed with the wonder of finding the love of her life here in Spain when she hadn't really wanted to be here at all, when she had intended spending her gap year back-packing around Europe, she had given his name, 'Diego Raffacani,' adding unnecessarily, 'He's Spanish.' Holding the fact that he was the most gorgeous-looking human being ever to walk the planet very close to her madly beating heart.

Ben had shot her the underbrow look that told her she was in for a lecture. 'How old is this guy? And I presume that, as you spend every day together, he's out of work?'

'Then you presume wrong!' Lisa's pointed chin shot up defensively. 'Diego works most evenings in one of the hotel restaurants down in Marbella—that's why he's free to spend his days with me! And, if you're really interested, he's twenty-two.'

Only four years her senior and so darkly handsome, so lithe and physically perfect that her heart ached just to look at him.

'So you've been picked up by a Spanish waiter,' Ben delivered drily. 'What a cliché!'

Unforgivably, Lisa giggled because, technically, Ben was spot on. She'd thought back to that day over three weeks ago. She'd spent the first week here dutifully tagging along with her friends. Descending from the hills where their rented ex-farmhouse holiday home was situated in the hired four-by-four. Doing what Ben and Sophie enjoyed. Playing golf, window-shopping, sipping coffee outside one of the trendy cafés, exploring what they could of the exclusive and highly fashionable nearby Puerto Banus area.

That particular day she'd cried off, the glitz beginning to pall, preferring to spend some time exploring the surrounding hilly back country on foot, comfortably clad in shorts and a matching acid-yellow T-shirt and sensible trainers. The buzzing of a motor scooter—a Vespino, Diego called it—was a warning that came too late. They had met on a bend in the steep, narrow track. Lisa had fallen backwards on to a carpet of wild herbs and the handsome young Spaniard had braked the scooter to a stone-spitting, slithering sideways halt.

Leaping across the narrow space, he'd gently helped her to her feet. So yes, he had quite literally picked her up! Looking into the concerned dark eyes, the proud, almost unnerving, aristocratic-looking features, at the tall bronzed perfection of a sensationally honed male clad just in patched cut-off denims that clipped the hard, narrow jut of his hips and a black vest top that had faded to grey, she had been utterly transfixed, her heart jumping up into her throat then spiralling down again to play havoc in the region of her stomach.

Their eyes had held as he assured himself she was unhurt—his questions couched in soft, only slightly accented English—gleaming black fringed with heavy thick lashes sending unspoken heady messages to wide inky-blue, the strong, steadying hands that curved around her slim shoulders transmitting a sensation that was a slow, unbearably sweet aching deep inside her.

That was how it had begun. And she would never again pour scorn on the idea of falling in love at first sight.

Ben had heaved a worried sigh, watching her as she made the morning coffee and Sophie, putting freshly picked peaches on a dish precisely in the centre of the breakfast table, had said lightly, 'Every girl's entitled to a holiday romance once in her life—provided things don't get out of hand.'

'They haven't, have they?' Ben put in quickly, his frown deepening.

As if she'd tell him! And no, they hadn't. Diego's kisses and caresses had sent her up in flames, the wanting a sweet wild torment inside her, but he had always pulled back at the critical moment, his voice soft and sultry as he had explained, 'You are very young, *querida*. One day you will be my bride. Until then, my angel, I value your purity above all else.'

'Is that a proposal?' Her voice was shaky with passion, her throat thick. He was all she had ever wanted; it was like a fairy tale.

'But of course, *querida*. You are my angel. I truly love you.' A gentle forefinger traced the outline of her lush lips, making her tremble. She could hardly speak through the rip-tide of ecstatic happiness, but managed a breathless, 'When?'

'When the time is right, *amor mio*,' he answered lightly, 'When you graduate from university—'

'That's years away!' she punched out, wriggling

out of his arms. He'd offered her heaven and now she could see it slipping away like water down a plughole.

He took her hands. 'There is no ending to our love; time won't alter that.' Warm, dark eyes smiled into hers. 'I too have things to do. Time will pass quickly, I promise. You will have vacations and I shall tell you where I am and you shall come to me.' His smile widened to a teasing grin. 'You have a rich daddy who will pay for your air fares!'

She dragged her hands away and sulked for the rest of the day. If he loved her as much as she loved him he wouldn't want to wait. Marrying her this minute wouldn't be soon enough!

But lying awake that night she'd formulated the perfect plan. She'd return to England at the end of their holiday as planned, square it with her father, who was remote enough not to mind what she did as long as she didn't bother him, and spend what was left of her gap year here with Diego. And at the end of the year they would have become so close, so loving, he wouldn't be able to face letting her go.

'Nothing to say for yourself?' Ben's question pulled her back into the farmhouse kitchen that day, almost four weeks ago. He accepted the mug of coffee she'd poured for him. 'I suppose you've told him who you are.'

'Of course he knows who I am!'

Ben's comment made no sense until he expounded, 'That your father is joint proprietor of a monthly glossy. That we publish *Lifestyle* among other less upmarket magazines. That our families are not short of cash.'

'There speaks the accountant!' Lisa derided gently. Ben had just finished a business accountancy course and on their return to England at the end of their holiday was to join the accounts department at *Lifestyle*.

'No,' Ben came back mildly. 'There speaks an old friend who is concerned for your happiness. Marbella is a hot spot of wealth; it attracts con men and hangers-on like flies. Men who latch on to rich women for what they can get out of them. Has your Spanish waiter wheedled anything out of you, by any chance?'

'Of course not!' But Lisa was aware that her cheeks burned with guilt. He hadn't wheedled that expensive watch out of her, she mentally defended. Far from it. He'd lost his own, explaining that the strap must have broken without him noticing it when he'd glanced at his naked wrist to check whether it was time for them to start heading back from the little secluded beach he'd taken her to.

That evening, while Sophie and Ben had been admiring the million dollar yachts in the marina, she'd slipped away and bought him a replacement, knowing he hadn't much money to spare. A waiter's wage wouldn't be anything to write home about and he needed a watch. 'And Diego doesn't like Marbella—' She wisely changed the subject. 'We never go there—he says it's too flashy, not the real Spain at all. We explore quaint little hill villages and off-the-track beaches.'

She loved Ben like a brother but was close to hating him for implying her beloved Diego was only interested in her for what he could get out of her. No way would she explain about the gift of that slim gold watch.

'So when do we get to meet him?' Sophie, the peace-maker, took her place at the table and reached for a crusty roll and the honey pot.

No answer, because there wasn't one to give. She'd once suggested a foursome—she'd wanted him to meet her best friends—but Diego had asserted that he was a selfish man and wanted her all to himself.

And now they were on their way to meet him at last—at his suggestion. Ben's comment had been a dry, 'He picked the most expensive joint he could find. I wonder who'll end up paying for the drinks and the meal!'

They were nearing the venue, the white futuristic hotel overlooking the gentle curve of the palm-fringed beach. Lisa's heart swelled. It would be all right; it had to be! Ben would take back every insulting insinuation when he realised what a super guy Diego was.

In a way she could understand his reservations. Ever since they'd been children he'd looked out for her. He still did, and that probably had something to do with her tiny stature—five-two, small-boned, delicately slender and wide-eyed. If she'd been built more like Sophie, tall and big in the bosom and hip department, he might have had more confidence in her ability to look out for herself.

Not that his opinion would make any difference to the way she felt about the man she was determined to marry. But she didn't want to quarrel with Ben; she was too fond of him.

'Hey, you guys—come and look at this!' Sophie cried. She'd been indulging in her favourite occupation, window-shopping, and was several yards behind them, her nose pinned to the window of a glitzy boutique. 'Would my bum look big in this?'

Ever willing to indulge his twin, Ben turned to retrace his steps, smiling, and Lisa stood where she was, too wound up to ooh and ahh over whatever it was Sophie was coveting.

Glancing at her platinum Jaeger-Le-Coultre watch, an eighteenth birthday gift from her father who thought that material things made up for a lack of any overt signs of parental affection, she noted there were still thirty minutes to get through before they were due to meet Diego. It felt like a lifetime.

The town was beginning to gear up for the evening, more people strolling the pavements, wanting to see and be seen, more flash cars cruising. One car in particular caught her attention. A bright scarlet drop-head sports job driven by a glamorous creature who looked as if she'd just materialised from between the covers of a high fashion magazine. But it was her passenger who drew her widening eyes—Diego? Surely not!

Diego, his thick dark hair expertly groomed, wearing classy casual chinos and an open-necked sleeveless shirt in a matching cool stone colour that accentuated the warm olive tones of his skin instead of the beat-up shorts and vest tops she was used to seeing him in.

The sports car growled to a halt, parked illegally outside the sort of jeweller's where the atmosphere would be too rarefied for ordinary mortals to breathe in, and Diego removed his arm from the back of the driver's seat and exited.

He had obviously smartened himself up for his meeting with them at the hotel and he looked good enough to eat, the darling! Like them, he was half an hour early. The classy female must have given him a lift. She was probably resident at the hotel where he worked, had recognised him as the waiter who serviced the table she regularly used and had picked him up.

The explanations flashed with comforting swiftness through her mind, though the phrase 'picked him up' did have uncomfortable connotations, thanks to Ben.

About to call his name, wave to attract his attention, she was morbidly glad she hadn't when he strolled round to the other side of the car, opened the door at the driver's side and helped the glamorous creature out, holding her hands. And not letting them go.

She was gorgeous. In spiky high heels, she was three inches short of his six-one, the hem of her silky black dress way above her knees, the costly fabric clinging to every curve of her eye-popping body, her bare arms glinting with, it seemed, half a ton of gold bracelets.

Jewelled hands slid from his fingers and snaked up to cup his face as he leaned towards her, saying something, his lips curved in the teasing smile Lisa knew all too well. Her heart stopped beating as the woman leaned right into him, bestowing kisses on one lean hard cheek and then the other before tipping her glossy head back, laughing up at him then leading him by the hand into the exclusive interior of the jeweller's shop.

As her heart crashed back into action Lisa went hot all over, then cold. Icy cold. Her breathing erratic, she felt giddy. There had to be a perfectly feasible explanation for what she had just witnessed. Anything else was unthinkable. Her dazed brain tried to find one.

Instead it spitefully reminded her that classy customers didn't go around kissing their waiters unless there was a high degree of intimacy between them. Then it made her recall her disbelief and disappointment when, the day before, he'd told her he wouldn't be able to see her that morning.

'Things to do,' he'd said, 'but we'll be meeting up in the evening.'

If she'd been a couple of years younger she would have thrown a tantrum. As it was, she'd been very adult about being deprived of his company on what he thought was her last day in Spain. She had meant to surprise him when she returned after she'd persuaded her father that she was going to spend her entire gap year holed up in Marbella. So she'd merely nodded, 'See you then,' as if not seeing him during the day didn't bother her.

Did 'Things to do', mean finding her replacement? If so, he'd hit the jackpot!

She shivered, swallowing down the sick feeling inside her, hating herself for thinking such a thing was possible. She rubbed a clammy hand over her forehead. It was all Ben's fault. He had put the idea of charismatic, handsome young Spaniards sucking up to wealthy lone female holiday-makers for what they could get out of them into her head.

'Practising being a statue?' Sophie slipped an arm under hers. 'You should have seen that suit! It was gorgeous but Ben said black wouldn't suit me and I'd have to live and sleep in it for fifty years to get my money's worth!'

'Typical boring accountant!' Lisa sniped, still annoyed with him for making her doubt—if only for a moment—her darling, adorable Diego.

'Now you know you don't mean that,' Sophie scolded mildly as they slowly, arm in arm, approached the wide flight of steps that led up to the hotel foyer. 'You know he can't help being practical any more than you can help being a dreamer. And cheer up, do. Such a long face! I can't wait to meet your Diego. It looks like he's serious about you if he wants to see me and Ben—your minders—on your last night in Spain!' She gave Lisa's arm a tiny, reassuring squeeze. 'I've told Ben not to say a word out of place; you know how protective he is of you. And I told him Diego probably wants to ask his permission—in the absence of your father—to visit you in England.'

Or to get a free slap-up meal and plenty to drink as a final perk. Lisa hated the disloyal thought that sprang into her head just as much as she hated her inability to prevent it forming. And loathed Ben for putting it there in the first place. She ousted it firmly. Diego wasn't into fancy food and wines. He'd always come provisioned with a picnic lunch on their days together. Crusty bread, olives, fruit and bottled water. Simple, cheap and wholesome.

'We're a bit early,' Ben commented as he caught up with them on the steps, eyeing the impressive smoked glass revolving doors.

'So?' Sophie shrugged. 'So we sit in the foyer, cool down and people watch.' She pushed through the doors and Lisa followed, wishing the dragging minutes away, desperate to ask Diego what he'd been doing with that devastatingly beautiful woman, why he'd let her kiss him, why they'd disappeared into that jeweller's together. Desperate to hear an entirely acceptable explanation.

And time, perversely, seemed to pass even more slowly in the air-conditioned space. All cool marble floors and stately columns, chandeliers and hushed opulence. Seated in matching pale jade-green upholstered chairs around a low table, Lisa had her back to the main area but Sophie was avidly scanning the languid comings and goings of the wealthy patrons.

'Now, how's that for an invitation!' Sophie giggled. 'Over there, by Reception—turn round and take a look. It's his lucky day!'

Lisa obliged. Anything to pass time, to stop her friends from wondering what was wrong with her, why she was wearing what they'd teasingly describe as her Tragic Face.

Diego and that woman!

Lisa shuddered with disbelief and a pain that wrapped icy fingers round her heart. What she was seeing wiped out every beautiful moment of the last weeks. Her eyes filled with tears. She blinked them away. One of his hands rested on the sexy curve of her black-silk-clad hip while the other flipped the lid of a small jeweller's box closed and slotted it into his pocket. A gold signet ring to match the watch she had bought him? Had the fabulous dark-haired woman already kitted him out with the classy casuals he was wearing?

Stretching up on her high spiky heels, the owner of the scarlet sports car reached up to whisper in his ear. Whatever she said made him grin, that wide slashing grin that said he was happy. She knew it so well!

A slender gold-dripping arm was lifted, beringed fingers dangling a room key in invitation, just before she turned and swayed away towards the bank of lifts, sexual confidence in every movement of those endless legs and delectable body. Diego watched her, still grinning, then turned and sauntered over to Reception.

'Steamy, or what?' Sophie hissed and Lisa had to summon every ounce of will-power to make her face blank as she turned back to face the others.

Ben kept glancing impatiently at his watch and Lisa said, trying not to sound as if her world had just fallen into ugly little pieces, 'Let's go and find a drink; I'm sick of sitting here.'

She shot to her feet to stall any protests from Sophie who was clearly enjoying her people watching session. And Ben followed suit but insisted on finding the disco bar, even though Lisa was convinced that Diego wouldn't turn up. Why would he, when he obviously had better prospects lined up? The betrayal was so immense she couldn't bear to think about it and she couldn't drag the others away from this place without confessing that Ben had been right about Diego.

Tapas and heavy beat music. Lisa demanded champagne. She would have asked for something strong enough to dull the piercing ache that stabbed through her heart—whisky, maybe—but she knew Ben wouldn't oblige. Convent educated by nuns strict enough to make your eyes water, treated like a vaguely annoying house guest by a father who had never taken much interest in her when she was home, Ben still tended to regard her as a delicate flower in need of perpetual care and attention.

'Yes, let's let our hair down,' Sophie put in when she noticed Ben's eyes gravitate to the soft drinks dispenser. 'It is our last night.'

Lisa drained her glass in two long thirsty swallows and sneaked a refill when Ben wasn't looking. He was peering at his watch.

Already ten minutes after the appointed time. Diego wouldn't be coming. Lisa was psyching herself up to tell them why, admit that Ben had been right about her Spanish waiter, drinking her second glass like water to dull the pain when Ben, watching her put the empty glass down on the tiny table, grinned at her. 'Dance, Lise?'

She wanted to dance about as much as she wanted to sit in a barrel of hot tar but anything had to be better than sitting here, getting tipsy, wanting to cry and doing her best not to, wanting to get her hands on Diego and strangle him after asking him how he could be so cruel.

She took Ben's hands and got to her feet. The floor dipped and heaved so, instead of dancing opposite him like the other couples, she clung on to his shoulders and was grateful when he clamped his hands around her waist to steady her. He raised his voice above the level of the thumping music and lectured, 'Squiffy, Lise? That will teach you not to drink a glass of champagne in five seconds flat.'

Two glasses, did he but know it! A hysterical giggle, halfway to a sob, caught in her throat. About to bury her head on his wide shoulder and confess everything, she saw Diego arrive. He said something to his glamorous new girlfriend who gave him a conspiratorial wink before sashaying off to the bar.

How dared he? How could he? Lisa knew she was about to be horribly sick. But she mustn't! Her fingers dug into Ben's shoulders. The pain in her gut was unbearable. Think about something else.

Revenge.

Show him! Show him that she wasn't a silly little girl with the smell of the schoolroom still lingering around her; that she wasn't the type to cry for a month because she'd been conned by an expert.

He was now standing a scant three feet away, his beautiful eyes lightly hooded as he watched her. What was his intention? How did such guys operate? Would he tap her on the shoulder, wish her a pleasant flight tomorrow, then join his new prey at the bar?

Or would he simply ignore her?

Well, he wouldn't ignore this—without giving herself time to think—her misery was too great to allow coherent thought—she lifted her hands, pulled Ben's head down and kissed him as if she were auditioning for a part in a blue movie.

And while Ben was trying to recover, his face brick-red, she looked into Diego's suddenly ferocious black eyes and lashed out, 'Go away! You're cramping my style!' and watched him turn abruptly on his heel, his mouth hard, his shoulders rigid, as he walked over to his new woman. Lisa thrust her knuckles into her mouth and bit them. She wanted to run after him, take it all back, beg him to make everything all right again.

But she knew she couldn't. The fairy tale romance was over, the ecstatic days when two hearts had seemed to beat as one had turned into a sordid nightmare.

She turned to Ben, her face white. 'Take me home. He won't be coming. I can explain. But not now. Take me home!'

CHAPTER TWO

SOMEONE was watching her. Lisa could actually and physically feel the dark power of unknown eyes on her. Nothing like the vaguely patronising glances she had endured all evening from the great and the good who were here in this glamorous setting to support and, far more importantly, be seen to support a fashionable charity.

She could feel the intensity of that look as it bored between her silk-clad shoulder blades. Feel the watchful, coldly cutting contempt.

It was unsettling, eerie.

A cold shiver flickered through her.

It was all in her imagination. It had to be!

Annoyed with herself, with the weariness that was making her prey to fanciful imagery, she did her best to dismiss it. She was overtired, that was all. It was obviously time to make tracks.

In her capacity as Sub for the Social Editor, as well as her own recently acquired title of Fashion Editor, she had noted the names and titles of those with the highest profiles and details of what the women were wearing. Neil, her snapper, had the shots. She'd dig him out from wherever he'd sloped off to and tell him to call it a day.

She was so tired her legs were having difficulty bearing her slight weight. If things at *Lifestyle* went on the way they were she'd find herself subbing for every department and working right round the clock eight days a week. Experienced editors were leaving in droves. Rats deserting the sinking ship, as her father said every time a letter of resignation landed on his desk.

The noise of high society at play had given her a pounding headache and she couldn't wait to get back to the peace and quiet of her flat. Trouble was, she was a round peg in a square hole and knew it. Perhaps that was responsible for the manic sensation of despising eyes following her every movement. She was transposing her own inner feelings on to a non-existent entity.

Of course no one was watching her, despising her! Why on earth would they?

Slender in her understated black sheath dress, she straightened her wilting spine and headed for the lavish buffet. Found Neil, as she'd thought she would, scoffing canapés as if he hadn't eaten for a fortnight.

'I'm off,' she said, shaking her head at his offer of wine. 'We've got all we need.' Though whether the tumbling circulation figures would be boosted by the feature in next month's issue was highly debatable.

Neil's brown eyes roamed her pale face. 'You look bushed. You should find yourself a proper job!' He abandoned the food in favour of a glass of red wine. 'Hang on a sec and I'll give you a lift home. I take it I'm invited to your engagement bash tomorrow night?'

'Of course. The more the merrier.' Lisa smiled then, her first genuine smile of the evening. A comforting warmth flooded through her, swamping out the unsettling sensation of being watched.

Dear Ben. She'd do her best to make him a good wife. No grand passion for either of them and that, they'd decided, was actually a bonus. There would be no ephemeral highs or debilitating lows in their relationship. They had discussed it, accepted it—embraced it, even. A safe marriage, a secure one, affection and respect on both sides was all either of them wanted. She didn't know about Ben but she guessed he was too pragmatic to harbour strong emotions; and as for her, well, the events of five years ago had put her right off the concept of passionate love. She would never again feel so deeply about anyone as she once had for the Spaniard. Which was a blessing. The stronger the emotions, the greater the hurt.

Unnervingly, the feeling of being watched came back again with a vengeance. She hated it; it scared her. It swamped all those comforting thoughts of Ben and the life they planned together.

She was out of here, home to get some much needed rest before her imagination ran away with her completely! 'I'll pass on that lift.' It was an effort to speak. 'I'll grab a taxi. See you.'

It was an even greater effort to turn. And impossible to stem her gasp of shock as she saw him. Cold black eyes watching her.

Just as she remembered him but with breath-snagging changes—a haughty elegance that made him seem older than his twenty-seven years, his dark, perfectly crafted suit adding to the intimidating effect, oozing the cool self-assurance of a man wholly at ease with himself.

The handsome features were arrogantly cold, the black eyes narrowed and intense as they raked the pallor of her face.

'Diego!' His name escaped her on a shaky huff of breath and everything inside her descended into chaos as he acknowledged her with a cool, dismissive dip of his dark head, turned on the heels of his immaculate, hand-crafted black leather shoes and walked away from her through the bejewelled, designer-clad chattering masses as if he didn't care to sully himself by any verbal contact.

Sophie was sprawled out on the sitting room sofa in the shoe box flat they shared near Clapham Common, her attractive face suffused with an enviable inner radiance until she glanced up on Lisa's arrival. 'God, you look awful!' She hauled herself into a sitting position. 'What happened? Did Neil make another pass at you? Shall I phone Ben and get him to go round and slap him?'

Lisa's mouth twitched. As usual, Sophie was completely OTT and she needed that to help her get the main event of the evening—seeing the man she had once believed to be the love of her life again—in proper perspective.

'No, nothing like that, thank heavens!' She lobbed her handbag to the floor and draped herself on to the armchair with the dodgy springs. 'These high society charity bashes are a complete pain.'

'Entirely your own fault,' Sophie pointed out unsympathetically. 'You should never have let yourself be talked into joining the staff. They tried to twist my arm too, remember, but I stuck out for my chosen career in physiotherapy.'

Lisa shrugged and kicked off her shoes. It was old history. She'd never got to university. On her return from Spain, joining her father in the service flat near the magazine's head office, he'd asked her to re-think her future.

The publishing company was in difficulties. They were in the process of downsizing, selling off or closing down the stodgy middle-of-the-road titles, concentrating on the flagship *Lifestyle*. They all had to tighten their belts. It was all hands on deck and loads of other clichés. It was her duty to join the staff—at peanut wages—and do what she could to help turn things around.

At the time she'd been too emotionally exhausted to stand up for what she wanted, in no state to really know what she did want any more.

'I expect you're right.' Lisa removed the battery of pins that kept her long blonde hair smoothly away from her face and was debating whether to tell her old friend of her sighting of Diego Raffacani when she noticed the champagne bottle and two flutes set out on the low coffee table. An arched brow tilted in Sophie's direction.

Sophie blushed then giggled. 'James proposed this evening. And I accepted.'

Lethargy entirely forgotten, Lisa leapt to her feet to give her friend a bear hug, settling beside her on the sofa, tucking her legs beneath her. 'That's the best news I've heard for longer than I can remember!' Sophie had been dating the attractive young GP for over a year and was madly in love with him. 'I'm so happy for you! Tell me more!'

'He's joining a practice in the West Country—all lovely and rural.' She stretched over for the bottle. 'He got called out, would you believe—so you're going to have to celebrate with me. I don't want to get squiffy on my own!'

The cork ricocheted all round the small room. 'We're going to have to house hunt down there,' Sophie confided excitedly. 'I can just see myself as a country doctor's wife—I'll have loads of babies, join the WI, put my name down for the church flower rota and wear tweed skirts and those green quilted waistcoat things. And hats! With pheasant feathers!'

'An unlikely scenario, if ever I heard one.' Lisa grinned, accepting a flute of bubbles, firmly dismissing the wish that she could be as excited over her own wedding plans as being well out of order. She and Ben weren't into high romance and magical, ephemeral flights of excitement. Companionship, mutual support… 'So when's the big day?' She rapidly blanked out another wholly unwelcome pang of envy.

'Three months. I'll be a midsummer bride.' Her eyes opened very wide. 'We could have a double wedding! That would be fantastic. Ben could move in here with you. It's time he got his act together and left the parental home.'

It was a possibility, Lisa mused as she listened to Sophie chatter on about wedding dresses, bridesmaids and honeymoon destinations.

Ben had mentioned a wait of a year after the official engagement announcement tomorrow. And he shared the family home in Holland Park for purely practical reasons. The money saved on rent and his keep was accumulating nicely. But when Sophie moved out she, Lisa, would still have to find the rent for this flat, so it would be both practical and sensible for Ben to share it as her husband.

After the second glass of champagne Lisa forgot practicalities and seemingly out of nowhere found herself blurting, 'He was at the charity bash tonight. Just as I remembered him, yet different.'

'Who?' Sophie, in mid flow over guest lists, refilled their glasses.

'Diego.'

How easily the name she hadn't mentioned since that dreadful night slipped from her tongue. How easily the sound of it brought it all back—the heartache, the anger, the sheer gut-wrenching misery, all the emotions she'd believed long dead and buried.

Fuelled by Sophie's blank look and an unaccustomed rapid intake of alcohol, she offered, 'Spain. You remember. That holiday you and Ben insisted on giving me?'

'Of course!' Sophie banged the side of her head with the heel of her hand. 'The handsome waiter you thought you were madly in love with, the one who dumped you on that last night—the snake! What a small world—and what was he doing mixing with that lot?'

'I've absolutely no idea.' Lisa put her glass down on the table, not really knowing why she'd started this, struggling to work out why she needed to talk about him. A catharsis maybe? An emotional release, setting her free from the pain of betrayal that had been buried deep within her psyche.

'He looked a million dollars—well, let's say he looked as if he'd regard that amount as small change. I guess his social-climbing career must have taken off in a big way.'

She had to say it, punch what he was firmly into her brain, paint him black so that never again would she—would she what? Still remember, still yearn, still dream about him?

'Blooming gigolo!' Sophie snorted. 'I hope you gave him an earful!'

'We didn't speak.' Just a single word. His name spilling from her lips.

'Probably just as well,' Sophie conceded. 'In your place I'd have probably walloped him and caused huge embarrassment all round. Now, let's forget about the wretch and talk about something nice—what are you planning on wearing for your party? I thought I'd wear the green satin—James says it turns him on…'

The Holland Park house looked at its festive best. Most of the guests were waiting when Lisa arrived. Flowers everywhere, filling the elegant rooms with the perfume of spring. Until her mother's death her parents had lived in a house similar to this, a scant five-minute walk away. She'd been at boarding school, barely fourteen years old, when the dreadful news had come.

Only after the funeral when her father had coolly informed her that he would be selling the family home, moving into a flat suitable for a man on his own, had the full enormity of her loss hit her. Her mother had loved her and now the sweet, gentle woman, who'd been completely dominated by the much stronger personality of her husband, was gone. Without consciously thinking it out she had naively believed that she and her father would now draw closer together in their mutual grief. But he was distancing himself even further, if that were possible, a fact brought home when he told her, 'The Claytons suggested you spend your school holidays with them. You've always got on well with the twins and Ben and Sophie will be far better company for you than I ever could be.'

Lisa closed her eyes briefly, willing the unwanted sadness of memories to leave her. This was a happy occasion, for pity's sake! Finding a smile, she handed her wrap to a waiting maid, who must have been hired for the evening, and went to find Ben.

The rooms were just comfortably crowded. Even so, her progress was slow, waylaid as she was by friends, colleagues and perfect strangers—invited by the elder Claytons, she guessed—who offered congratulations.

Items of furniture had been pushed to the edges of the rooms or removed entirely and a sumptuous buffet had been laid out on the long dining room table, attended by smartly uniformed waiters. Ben and his parents were grouped by one of the tall windows, seemingly in private, earnest conversation. A conversation which ended abruptly when Lisa reached Ben and touched the sleeve of his dinner jacket to claim his attention.

'Is something wrong?' she asked, her silky brows drawing together. All three of them looked strangely worried but Honor Clayton denied immediately, 'Of course not! How nice you look, dear. Doesn't she, Ben? Is Sophie with you? How like you two girls to be late!'

'She's waiting for James. He's picking her up at the flat and bringing her here. She wanted them to arrive together.' Lisa tucked her hand beneath Ben's arm. 'I gather you've heard her news?' She knew Honor had. She'd been there when Sophie had put the phone down after speaking to her mother, seen the wry twist of her mobile mouth, the slight shrug accompanying the upward roll of her eyes.

Honor lifted her heavy shoulders in a gesture of resignation. 'Of course. But do I see her as the wife of a humble country GP?' She did her best to smile. 'Time will tell, I suppose.'

'She's very happy,' Lisa said gently. Her future mother-in-law was a snob but she meant well. She would never forget the rather self-conscious heartiness with which the older woman had received her on those long ago school holidays after her mother's death.

Young as she'd been at the time, she had instinctively known that Honor hadn't the words to console the motherless child of her husband's business partner and had resorted to booming exhortations: 'Now twins, find something jolly to do with little Lisa—no slouching about indoors and getting bored and miserable! There are plenty of things to do in London. Cinemas, parks…'

Into the edgy silence that had fallen following her last statement—though why the family should be uneasy about a guy like James being admitted to their ranks, Lisa couldn't begin to fathom—she asked, 'Where's Father?'

Again the odd sensation of unease. Arthur Clayton glanced initially at his son and then his wife. He spoke for the first time since Lisa had joined them. 'He's with our top advertiser in the study. He shouldn't be long. It's not ideal—a private family celebration and all that. But apparently his time in the UK is extremely limited.'

'And we've been nattering away for far too long,' Honor said bracingly. 'Time to circulate. Come, Arthur! You can make your speech as soon as Lisa's father appears—and I presume he'll want to say a few words of his own to mark the occasion. Everyone here knows, of course, but we have to make the engagement official.' Smiling fixedly, she dragged her husband into the main reception rooms and Lisa asked, 'Something's wrong, isn't it, Ben? At first I thought your parents were unhappy about Sophie's wedding plans. But it's not that, is it?'

'Problems over advertising revenue,' he confessed, keeping his voice down, uneasy about being overheard. 'But nothing for you to worry about, old thing. Is that dress new? It looks as if it cost a fortune.' He changed the subject, not wanting to pursue it there, a slight frown pulling his brows together as glanced at the elegant creation she was wearing. A slip dress in pale coffee-tinted layered chiffon decorated with swirling patterns of toning sequins, the bodice held up by narrow sequined straps.

Her fingers slid away from his arm as she waited for the unwarranted spurt of anger to die down. He had always been ultra careful about money, she knew that and, far from irritating her, she had seen the character trait as vaguely amusing. She didn't expect him to change, of course she didn't, but it would have been nice if he'd complimented her on her appearance before niggling about how much the dress had cost.

Dismissing her reaction as absurd—they didn't have the type of relationship that demanded sloppy compliments—she gave him a slight smile of conspiracy. 'It's hired for the evening—but don't tell anyone!'

She accepted the reward of his grin, the warm hand that slid around her tiny waist, with a small curve of her lips, a dimpling cheek. But there was more. 'Don't patronise me, Ben. If we have money problems I should know about them.' Number crunching was his department, not hers; he didn't interfere with her editorial input, but this was different.

Ben hunched his shoulders uncomfortably and for a moment Lisa believed he wasn't going to enlighten her. Then he shot her a wry glance. 'We didn't want to worry you. After all, your father might talk him round.'

'Who?'

'The top guy at Trading International. He's threatening to withdraw the company's advertising.'

'And that's serious?'

'You bet your sweet life it is! High fashion leather wear, the *Los Clasicos* range of jewellery, wine, gourmet cheeses, luxury hotels and apartments worldwide. Withdraw that lot and we're up the creek without a paddle.'

'That bad.' Lisa sucked her lower lip between her teeth. Shouldn't she have seen this coming? What major advertiser would stick with a magazine with circulation figures in slow and seemingly unalterable decline? 'What chance is there of Father talking him around?'

Ben shrugged. 'God knows!' He drew her away from the window. 'I shouldn't have told you—don't let it spoil our evening, Lise. If everything goes pear-shaped and *Lifestyle* folds, we'll be OK. With my qualifications and your experience we'll find other work. Hold that thought while we mingle.'

Smiling, chatting, doing her best to act as if all was right with her world, Lisa felt hollow inside, her eyes straying continually to the study, where her father was trying to persuade a hard-nosed business mogul not to pull the plug. Many of the guests tonight were on the staff of *Lifestyle*. By this time next month they could all be out of work, her father and Arthur Clayton looking into the bleak face of failure.

How could Ben possibly expect her to dismiss all that from her mind and console herself with the thought that he and she would be OK?

He couldn't be that selfish, could he? She shook her head in instinctive negation. Of course not. He'd only said that in an effort to cheer her up, not wanting their special evening to be spoiled for her.

As she accepted a flute of champagne someone put into her hand she saw her father and her heart banged against her breastbone.

It was impossible to tell from his expression whether or not he'd been successful. As always, her father kept his feelings to himself.

Silence fell, as if the sheer presence of the man had commanded it. When he spoke, talking of his happiness at the further cementing of the relationship between the two families, the words went in one ear and straight out of the other. And when Ben slid the diamond hoop on her wedding finger her face ached from smiling and the growing applause, the chorus of Ooohs and Aaahs, the glasses raised in cheerful toasts, slid past her consciousness, leaving no ripples at all.

All she was aware of was her father's stern features, the rigid set of his shoulders. He was standing just beyond the chattering group surrounding her and Ben. One tight-jawed sideways inclination of his head had her murmuring her excuses and threading her way towards him.

Taking the champagne glass from her fingers he said, 'You are needed in the study.'

'Me?' Lisa noted the impatient tightening of his thin mouth at what he would see as her idiotic questioning of his perfectly plain statement and to deflect the sarcastic comeback she knew from experience was in store for her she hurriedly asked, 'How did it go? Ben told me there were problems.'

What could the big-shot want with her? An assurance that she had a pile of must-read, breathtakingly fascinating articles in her in-tray? The sort of stuff that would guarantee a huge upsurge in readership? As if! Anything remotely startling or contentious would be immediately scotched at editorial meetings by the partners.

Skirting her question, Gerald Pennington remarked coolly, 'As I said, you seem to be needed. As far as I can tell, all you can do is try not to make matters worse. It shouldn't take long and then you can enjoy the rest of your evening.'

Yeah, right, Lisa thought resignedly as she went to answer the summons. Her hand on the study door, she paused for a moment, psyching herself up to deliver the spiel of her life. If she could make the future editorial input sound really cutting edge maybe she could swing the balance in their favour. Though 'cutting edge' didn't gel with anodyne accounts of boring society gatherings or fashion articles aimed solely at the seriously wealthy.

If she messed up her father would never forgive her. Not for the first time she wondered why she bothered to try to please him, why she wanted what she had never had—the warmth of his approval.

Wrinkling her neat nose, pushing her relationship with her father to the back of her mind, she straightened her spine, plastered a smile on her face and walked into the study.

And he was there, leaning against the edge of Arthur Clayton's desk, his long, immaculately trousered legs crossed at the ankles, black eyes cold and hard, narrowed on her face.

Her stomach jumped in shock. 'There has to be a mistake.' Her voice sounded echoey through the buzzing in her ears. She took a step backwards, one hand outstretched as she felt for the door. Coming face to face with Diego Raffacani last night had been bad enough, stirring painful memories back to life. But here—posing as a major advertiser—

'No mistake, I assure you. Sit down, Miss Pennington.'

He edged fully upright, feet apart, long-fingered hands resting on narrow hips, the jacket of his suit parting to reveal a matching waistcoat smoothly clinging to his powerful torso. The picture of sartorial elegance—no sign of the slightly shabby, casually dressed and ultra laid-back Spanish lover who had broken her heart.

The formality of his address helped her to pull herself together. It had been a long time. Too long to allow memories to live, festering away in the dark, rarely visited regions of her mind. If he had changed—and she only had to look into that hard, classically handsome face to know that he had—then so had she.

She watched him take Arthur's swivel chair behind the desk, her heart thumping at the base of her throat. He still moved with the same inborn grace and she couldn't help remembering how she had adored watching him.

Lisa took the chair opposite and sat, her hands loosely clasped together in her lap. Seeking the defence of outward composure, her voice commendably calm, she asked, 'So you now work for Trading International?' reining back the snide comment that it was a big step up for a humble waiter. For everyone's sake she couldn't afford to rub him up the wrong way, even though she still longed to wring his neck for what he had done to her!

'Since my father's retirement, I am Trading International.' He placed his elbows on the arm rests of the chair he was using, steepling his fingers, the tips lightly touching his wide, sensual mouth, narrowed eyes watching the disbelief and then the obvious shock flicker across her face.

The face of an angel. The smile of a siren. And the sensitivity and morals of an alley cat!

She was more beautiful than he remembered, the delicate perfectly formed body still unbelievably sexy.

Five years ago he could have taken that body, it had been his for the asking. He narrowed his eyes, black gleaming through the enigmatic, heavy sweep of his lashes. Five years ago he had denied himself the sensual pleasure of the ultimate possession of the bewitching temptation of her. Now, one way or another, he was going to have her. Take what he wanted for as long as he wanted it, learn the secrets of her delectable body then toss her back where she belonged.

Dropping his hands, he leaned further back in the chair, idly pondering the pleasure of removing the clasp that maintained the sophisticated upsweep of her hair and seeing the silvery silky mass tumble down to the creamy skin of her naked shoulders and the gentle, inviting curve of her breasts.

His accent was slightly more pronounced than was usual, his tone smooth as cream, he imparted, 'I have a proposition to put to you, Miss Pennington…'

CHAPTER THREE

'YOU can't mean that!'

It was appalling, utterly crazy! As propositions went it was totally unbelievable—she must have misheard. Either that or Diego Raffacani had gone stark staring mad!

Her wildly churning emotions swept away the last fragile pretence of composure and Lisa pushed herself to her feet, then wholeheartedly wished she hadn't. Her body was trembling so badly she was swaying on her kitten heels. Her breath shortened and her inky-blue eyes widened, darkening to black as she watched him get to his own feet and move around the desk to stand beside her.

Her nostrils flared as she inhaled the scent of him, the heat of his body. Her mouth ran dry and her heart began to pound as she stared up into the lean powerful face, watched the sinfully sensual line of his mouth as he asserted, 'I meant every word,' and dropped back into the chair she had vacated as her knees finally buckled beneath her.

'Why?' Her voice croaked as her mind skittered back and forth over everything he'd said. It was impossible to keep a sensible or decisive thought in her head for more than a nanosecond.

'Because you owe me.' His teeth glinted white. 'Five years ago you were more than willing. But out of respect for your youth and what I then believed to be your inexperience I held back. You proved yourself unworthy of any man's respect.' His hard, beautiful face was rigid with contempt. 'I loved you but you threw it back in my face—that was my reward for my unselfish consideration. It is now time to pay your debt to me. Six months, or maybe even three, should be enough to get you out of my system.' There was a glint in his eyes, a twist to his mouth that sent a waterfall of ice skittering down her backbone as he drawled, 'If you prick a Spaniard's pride then you sit back and wait for the inevitable vengeance.'

Lisa shuddered as a knot of something tight and hot claimed her stomach. She raised her shaky hands to cover her mouth, fighting to come to terms with what he was demanding of her. Grappling to make some sense of the situation, she seized on one solid fact and accused, 'You said you were just a waiter. And all the time you were rotten rich! You lied!'

His mouth flat he turned away from her. 'I didn't lie to you. You simply made your own interpretation. You were happy to amuse yourself with what you saw as a no-account stud. You were at a loose end and looking for a cheap holiday romance. You wanted sex. I didn't oblige so you eased your frustration by sleeping with the man I now know to be Ben Clayton.'

'For pity's sake!' Hot colour swept her face. 'I was only dancing—how dare you?'

Resuming his seat on the opposite side of the desk, he slashed his hand imperiously, cutting off any further words of self-justification. 'You were crawling all over him, kissing him. And if you don't recall what you said to me, I do.'

Lisa cringed away from the savage glitter of his midnight eyes. Of course she remembered. She remembered every word they had ever said to each other. And, as for the last vile words she had ever spoken to him… Well, she had no defence, certainly none that he would listen to. Prick a Spaniard's pride…

'The offer's on the table,' he said with a snap in his voice that made Lisa feel as if she'd just been pronounced terminally ill. 'You live with me, lie with me, pleasure me until you bore me. In return I will not cancel my company's advertising and use one of your competitors. I will even buy in, bring in new blood to gloss up *Lifestyle*'s dull image, bring it back to success. If you refuse, as is your right, of course, then—' With a slight shrug of those impressive shoulders he allowed the threat to hang in the air—air that now seemed to be suffocatingly thick and heavy.

Lisa couldn't breathe. Her brain wasn't functioning as it should. She could only hear the words that had burned themselves into her mind—'lie with me, pleasure me'—and only wonder with helpless self-loathing at the way the responsive heat pooled between her thighs and a piercing awareness made her whole body tremble. After all this time he could still reach her. How many times had she told herself that he wasn't worth wasting a single thought on? Millions! And yet she only had to be near him—

'I've only just got engaged,' she pushed out between suddenly unbearably sensitised lips, knowing that he would regard the statement as irrelevant.

'Break it.'

He got to his feet, large, lean and intimidating. But so utterly gorgeous her mouth went dry as she looked at him, searching for the man he had been, the man she had fallen so helplessly in love with.

'I'll call on you tomorrow morning. Early. For your decision.'

Diego strode out of the room, closing the door behind him with an emphatic snap. Lisa shuddered, wrapping her arms around a frame that seemed about to shake itself to pieces. Bereft of his presence, the room felt cold and hollow. But then, she thought shakily, he had always generated an atmosphere so vital the air around him was charged with stinging sexual energy. Unfortunately nothing had changed in that respect.

She felt sick with nervous tension. What Diego had asked—demanded—of her was impossible! Quelling the uncomfortable knowledge that he need only have used a kind word, confessed, with regret, that he had been two-timing her all those years ago, then the impossible would have turned into the opposite, she gave herself a savage mental shake.

Like the arrogant swine he obviously was he was accusing her of being in the wrong. True, she had behaved atrociously. But she had been too young to cope with his betrayal with any dignity at all. She'd had too much to drink, been borderline hysterical...

'So, how did it go?'

Lisa nearly leapt out of her skin. She'd been

drowning in her own tortured thoughts and hadn't heard Ben enter. He placed a hand on her shoulder. 'I saw Señor Raffacani leave—now, why does that name ring a bell?' He hunched his shoulders, dismissing it as unimportant. 'Don't suppose you talked him out of withdrawing his advertising account with us?' he queried defeatedly. 'The Dads couldn't get anywhere with him, apparently.'

At the wry resignation in his tone Lisa scrambled to her feet. His brows peaked in enquiry. He carried no sizzling sexual aura around with him. Just stolid, quietly comfortable normality. For the first time ever she wanted to fling herself into his arms and beg him to save her from the old treacherous longings Diego had woken within her. But they didn't have the kind of passionate relationship that would make that possible. For years now she'd tried her best to appear coolly sophisticated, in control. He would hate it if she went to pieces.

Her eyes stung with tears and she bent to adjust a strap on one of her shoes to hide them. Dear practical, sensible Ben would be mortified if he thought she was even considering—for one split second—prostituting herself to save the magazine.

But she wasn't, was she? she adjured herself silently. No way! Not ever! She straightened, willing herself to appear normal. 'We can't talk about it now. Later. We can stay another half an hour then you can take me home and we'll discuss it.'

A look of incredulity spread across his pleasant features. 'The Dads will want to know what he said to you, you know they will. We can't just walk out of our own party. People will think it's odd, to say the least!'

'No, they won't.' Lisa sighed resignedly, pointing out, 'They'll think we're like all newly engaged couples—panting to be alone together.'

'Don't be crude, Lise—it doesn't suit you.' His frown deepened. 'And why all this cloak-and-dagger stuff? Either the guy's going to finish with us, or he isn't. A straight yes or no will do.'

Ignoring his reprimand—there had been no driven eagerness in their desire to be alone together so he wouldn't understand what she'd been getting at—she tucked her hand beneath his arm and explained heavily, 'It's not as simple as that. Raffacani made a proposition. With strings attached. I need to tell you about them, in private, before everything comes crashing down round our heads.'

That earned her a puzzled glance but stopped him arguing and they rejoined the party. And for the entire fifteen minutes or so while they mingled and chatted Lisa's head felt as though her brains had been scrambled, the hopelessness of the situation making her stomach cramp and her heart bang against her ribs.

She had it in her power to save her colleagues' jobs, ensure them a brighter, more secure future. One word from her would prevent Arthur Clayton and her father from looking into the bleak face of failure. She owed them something, didn't she?

A light hand on her shoulder had her tensing her spine but it was only Maggie Devonshire, the Picture Editor. 'Caught you at last!' Her kindly face beamed with pleasure. 'I'm so happy for both of you—two young things starting out together, that's so beautiful!' Ready tears misted her tired hazel eyes. 'Show me the ring.'

As Lisa put her hand into the older woman's her own eyes stung. Maggie was one of the best; she bore her troubles with fortitude and grace. Her son had suffered brain damage at birth; Billy had the mind of a four-year-old in a young man's body. Because Maggie's husband had walked out on her many years ago she coped on her own, delivering Billy to the day care centre on her way to work, collecting him on her way home. And never one self-pitying word. If she lost her job she would never find another. In her mid-fifties all she could hope for would be something low paid and menial—cleaning offices, maybe.

A clammy chill spread over every inch of her body as Maggie, her admiration of the diamond hoop voluble, released her hand and confided, 'It was lovely of you to invite me but I really must be off. Billy's spending the evening with a neighbour. I don't want to impose on her good nature. You never know, I might need her again. A handsome millionaire might ask me out to dinner!'

As she turned away with a light self-mocking laugh Lisa put an unsteady hand on Ben's arm. 'Let's go,' she murmured thickly.

Could she barter her body for the sake of the magazine and the jobs it provided? And why did thinking about exactly what that would entail send dark heat surging through her veins?

She would have to return Ben's ring. How hurt would he be?

Could a short affair—how long would it be before Diego decided she bored him?—leave her anything other than deeply humiliated?

Even more deeply humiliated than she felt right now, she decided, angry with herself as her skin began to flutter and her heartbeat quicken at the mere thought of making love with Diego Raffacani.

'You will do as he asks?'

Slumped on the sofa, the coffee she'd made cold on the table in front of him, Ben had listened to all she'd had to say in heavy silence. Now he waited for an answer to his question.

Lisa, pacing back and forth, driven by a gripping inner tension, couldn't find one and only came to an abrupt, shocked standstill when Ben stated flatly, 'You want to. You still want him. Five years ago you swore you were madly in love with him. Sophie and I thought it was teenage infatuation. None of us knew who he really was and I put the worst possible interpretation on the whole thing. I thought he was stringing you along for what he could wheedle out of you.' His shoulders hunched in a wry shrug. 'When he didn't turn up that night I assumed that was the end of it, but it obviously wasn't.'

'He did turn up,' Lisa admitted unhappily, wondering why Ben wasn't furiously angry over Raffacani's proposition, vowing to kill the other man if he ever came near her again. Wondering, too, why his pragmatic response didn't hurt her.

Gingerly, she perched on the edge of the sofa beside him. 'That last night he turned up with a totally fabulous woman—rich as Croesus, by the look of her.' She didn't mention those earlier sightings; there seemed little point. 'I was sick with jealousy. I wanted to pay him back. So I kissed you, remember?'

'Do I!' He shifted uncomfortably. 'You shocked me rigid. That sort of behaviour in a public place was so unlike you. It was months before I could feel really easy in your company after that.'

Ignoring the evidence of his streak of prudery, Lisa confessed, 'Diego was standing right behind us. I said something really vile to him. That's why he's put such impossible strings on his rescue package. To punish me. I hurt his precious pride.'

Ben swung his head round to look at her. Something about that look told her he was resigned to letting her go, she thought in a panic, knowing that even though they weren't in love with each other he represented emotional safety. 'Not impossible, surely? You obviously hurt more than his pride,' he said gently. 'Five years is a long time for a man like him to carry a torch.'

'Don't be ridiculous!' Lisa dismissed sharply. 'I told you—he wants to punish me.'

'And you want that kind of punishment?'

'Of course not!' she denied, her cheeks going hot at the thought of the kind of punishment Diego could dole out.

'Then why didn't you tell him straight out to sling his hook? Why feel you had to discuss the situation if you were unwilling to go along with it? And don't repeat all that other stuff—saving *Lifestyle* and all that. If it folds it wouldn't be the end of the world.

The Dads would sink into comfortable retirement and I could find other work in my field, no problem—'

'And what about the others? Their jobs would go. And Maggie—what would she do?' she interrupted heatedly, incensed that he should put her concerns down to hot air and a sneaky desire to do exactly what Diego had suggested.

'People are made redundant every day,' he pointed out. 'They don't starve to death. They manage. And, as for Maggie, she's nearing retirement age. She'll receive a worthwhile pension.'

He huffed out his breath and got slowly to his feet. 'Admit it, Lise. You'd be a willing sacrificial lamb. You and I never pretended to a grand passion. If, deep down, you're still in love with your Spaniard, then go to him. But be honest about it, don't dress it up as anything other than a need to be with him at any cost.' He put his hand on her shoulder and gave it an affectionate squeeze. 'Think about it and be honest with yourself. And, if you do decide to do as he asks, you have my blessing. I don't go for all that hearts and flowers stuff, you know that. Even so, I wouldn't want a wife who was secretly yearning for another man. It wouldn't work out.' He gave her a last gentle smile. 'Keep the ring as a symbol of my regard for you.'

Lisa never was sure how long she sat there after Ben walked out. She was frozen with shock. How easily he'd let her go. How pertinently he'd put his finger on the heart of the matter. She still wanted Diego, was still in love with the handsome, charismatic young Spaniard who had broken her heart all those years ago

She had never regarded herself as a fool, but she did now.

Wearily, she dragged herself to her room, unwilling to face Sophie. Closing the door behind her, she leant against it, pressing her fingertips to her throbbing temples.

Diego would demand her decision in the morning.

Would she be strong enough, sane enough, to tell him to get lost? Leave *Lifestyle* to its ignominious fate. As Ben had pointed out, it wouldn't be the end of the world if the magazine folded; saving it would just be her excuse to justify her actions. A willing lamb to the slaughter.

Or would she go with him, lie with him and pleasure him? Take what she could of him and bear the pain and shame when it was over? Could she resist the wicked temptation?

Exiting the taxi that had brought him from the central London hotel he was using, Diego instructed the driver to wait. This wouldn't take long.

Despite his immaculate cashmere overcoat he shivered, blamed the miserable English March weather and set his jaw grimly. The unprecedented stinging, shivery sensation deep inside him had nothing to do with her answer.

It was down to the depressing weather, the grey streets and buildings, so unlike his vibrant, colourful homeland that it made his very soul shake inside him.

Or he'd caught flu—that would explain the band of perspiration that was chilling on his forehead.

His long mouth quirked wryly. He was turning into a hypochondriac now!

Shrugging that distasteful notion aside, he pushed open the door of what had once been an elegant Regency townhouse and was now converted into tiny flats. The unfurnished hallway was bleak. Someone's bicycle leant against the banisters of the uncarpeted stairs. His heart jumped like a landed fish as he began to mount them but he refused to let the possibility of a negative answer to his proposition take root in his mind.

Five years ago, when he'd truly loved her, she'd been greedy for sex, he reminded himself forcefully. It had taken all his self-control to deny her. He'd known his own mind, wanted her as he'd never wanted another woman, but she'd been young and impressionable and he'd needed her to be as sure as he was. Out of respect for her he'd denied himself the rapture of making love with her, so on that last hateful night she'd set her sights on Clayton, dismissing the supposedly penniless waiter as if he were dirt beneath her dainty feet.

Greedy for sex then—nothing would have changed over the intervening years. No problem there, then. Giving in to his demands for retribution would be no hardship as far as she was concerned—with the added, not inconsiderable bonus of the financial security engendered by the renaissance of *Lifestyle*. That would be important to her. Despite her initial, and understandable, shocked protests she'd had all night to think her way round his proposition. Lisa Pennington would always come out in favour of what was best for her.

He had her! He was damn sure of it!

His hands flexed into fists as his body leapt and hardened at the remembrance of her eager, passionate responses all those years ago. How he'd adored her, the blind witchery of falling truly in love for the first time in his life making him romanticize her, believing her to be an angel sent from heaven for him alone.

Cretino!

He gritted his teeth. Reaching the second floor landing, standing before the door to the flat she occupied, his mind darkened with an unaccustomed flicker of self-doubt.

Clayton.

Had she already given the poor guy his marching orders? Was he even now nursing a broken heart? He remembered, all too clearly, exactly how he'd felt that night five years ago. That night and countless sleep-deprived others. The pang of sympathy shook him. Then, determinedly, he dismissed it.

Lisa Pennington was a hussy. In the long run he'd be doing Clayton a huge favour.

He lifted his hand and pressed the doorbell.

CHAPTER FOUR

HER usually welcome morning tea tasted vile. Lisa put the cup down on the cramped breakfast bar; she couldn't stomach another drop.

She hadn't slept, hadn't expected to. And how early was 'early'? she asked herself agitatedly.

At least Sophie wouldn't be around when Diego arrived for his answer. It had been well after three when she'd heard the other girl's exaggeratedly careful progress to her bedroom, so she'd probably sleep in until eleven or even later. It was Sunday, after all, the day they usually spent relaxing, tackling the most pressing chores, catching up on the gossip.

She moved to the sitting room, restless. There would be nothing usual about today.

Crunch time.

Her heart lurched.

Would she? Wouldn't she?

Tugging her aubergine-coloured sweatshirt down over her jeans-clad hips she gravitated to the mirror that hung over the blocked-off fireplace. What she saw did nothing for her self-assurance. She looked like a twelve-year old, she decided, sighing with disgust.

The baggy top swamped her delicate curves. She looked flat as a board. Her hair scraped back off her face, held into her nape with a limp ribbon, looked dull and lifeless. As did the dark-ringed eyes that stared mournfully back at her.

Quelling the sudden impulse to go and do something about the way she looked, she turned and paced back to the kitchen. She had no wish to impress him. In fact, if she looked like a rag doll who'd been left out in the rain he might decide he wanted nothing to do with her and take back that shameful proposition, take the decision she'd been wrestling with all through the wretched night right out of her hands.

Perhaps if she ate something the horrible shaky feeling inside her would go away. But one look at her cooling cup of tea made her feel queasy and she scotched the idea of trying to eat anything, jumping like a scalded cat when the doorbell rang.

He was here!

And she still hadn't decided what answer to give him. Ben had made her take a long hard look at her motivations for even considering, for a single second, Diego's blackmailing proposition. The conclusions she'd drawn had told her uncomfortable things about herself. She knew what she wanted but couldn't convince herself that it would be right for her or for Diego.

A shriller, more persistent ring of the doorbell had her scurrying out of the kitchen on legs that felt as insubstantial as cotton wool. The noise would wake Sophie and that would be disastrous. She was going to have to pick her words carefully when she told her best mate that her engagement to her beloved twin was off. And explain why. Ben wouldn't put himself through the humiliation of marrying a woman who, so he'd decided, was still in love with another man.

Her hands were shaking as she opened the door and met Diego's impatient dark eyes. Her breath locked in her lungs and a sharp, catching sensation invaded her stomach. No man had the right to be so out and out gorgeous, so—so shatteringly male. Once she had rejoiced in his masculine perfection—now the slightly older, tougher version scared her witless!

Wordlessly she stood aside to allow him to enter, noting the elegantly styled coat he wore with the careless arrogance of a man born to such luxuries.

Once, in those long-ago days of heady loving, she had believed him penniless, scraping a meagre living while she had come from a well-heeled family. His imagined near poverty hadn't bothered her a jot; now his obvious wealth gave her the shivers. Her once adored Diego was a stranger.

Watching him slide his eyes dismissively over the mediocre contents of the sitting room, she searched for something, anything, of the charismatic young Spaniard who had claimed her loving heart for his own during that long, glorious summer five years ago. And found none. Nothing in his narrowed-eyed inventory of her appearance, not a flicker on that lean, hard face to remind her of the way he had once loved her.

Had seemed to love her, she reinforced tiredly. Nothing about the younger Diego Raffacani had been as it seemed. In that bleak moment she reached her final decision.

'Well?'

The harsh monosyllable made her stomach turn right over. Long fingers drew back his cuff as he consulted his watch in a gesture she was sure was meant to intimidate her into blurting an immediate answer. The watch he wore wasn't the one she had given him. That had been slim and gold; the one he wore now was dark and chunky. So why did that hurt so much?

Grabbing on to the last ragged remnants of her composure, she said thinly, 'It looks cold out. I'll make coffee.' Letting him know this was her home and she wasn't about to be intimidated into anything. But really, she silently admitted with painful honesty as she walked back into the tiny kitchen, it was to put off the time when she would sell the magazine down the river, lose her colleagues their jobs. It was on her conscience but, as Ben had said, it wouldn't be the end of the world.

The underlying reason for her delaying tactics, of course, was more visceral. Once she'd told him where to put his 'proposition' she would never see him again. It shouldn't hurt, shouldn't make her feel empty and only half alive. But it did.

As the door closed behind her Diego made a determined effort to get his head straight. Seeing her this morning, pale and waif-like, bereft of the classy dress she'd been wearing the night before, her milky skin innocent of make-up, he'd experienced a near savage need to take her out of her dreary surroundings, take her to the sun, pamper her, care for her, see those huge drowning inky-blue eyes come alive, laughing and vital. Smiling for him as once they had used to, making him feel like the luckiest man in the world.

How crazy could a man get?

Despite appearances, she was as vulnerable as an armoured tank. He wouldn't let a pang of misplaced compassion rob him of a vengeance he'd been planning ever since he'd learned that *Lifestyle* was sliding unstoppably downhill.

Lisa Pennington could look out for herself, could take a man's love and throw it back in his face. He had no doubt she'd frittered her time away at university, batting those fabulous lashes at any male student who took her fickle fancy.

Gritting his teeth against the invasive spurt of anger—not jealousy, of course not—he paced the narrow room. Had she finally decided to marry that poor sucker, Clayton, because she'd seen him as a meal ticket? Probably. By the look of her surroundings she wasn't doing well financially. Nepotism had undoubtedly been responsible for her finally ending up on the magazine.

Despite her engagement, she would ditch Clayton. Having sex without love wouldn't be a problem for her, would it? He knew her track record. Even at just turned eighteen she'd been greedy for it and when he'd behaved honorably, out of love and respect for her, she'd turned to the nearest male who would oblige. Clayton.

Grimacing, he cursed under his breath. Memories of that last night still haunted his dreams. But he had her now; he was sure of that.

Denying the restless energy that was forcing him

to pace the cheap carpet he sank down on to the arm-chair. He closed his eyes, savouring the victory to come, the final and definitive act of removing her from his system, leaving him free at last to find pleasure, satisfaction and contentment with a woman who would be worthy to share the rest of his life, give him children.

There was no way Lisa Pennington would turn his offer down. With *Lifestyle* thriving again—and he could make that happen—her doting daddy could be relied on for fat handouts and she wouldn't have to worry about working for her living.

He liked his coffee strong, black and sugarless, she remembered as she placed a single earthenware cup and saucer beside the cafetière on the tray. Her hands were shaking. Courage, she told herself as she pulled in a sharp breath and walked out of the kitchen. Get it over with.

Maybe she was being selfish in letting *Lifestyle* fold but, as Ben had pointed out, no one would starve. The staff would find other work and Maggie, her main concern, would receive a pension.

The other way, selling her body for Diego to use until he tired of the game, would do her irreparable damage. And she knew it wouldn't do Diego much good either. Oh, right now he thought revenge would taste sweet, she understood that. But somewhere behind the coldly handsome mask he wore there had to be vestiges of decency. He would end up hating himself for what he had done.

Or would he?

He hadn't behaved decently five years ago, had he? Thinking of the woman he'd been with turned her stomach. And yet he blamed her for what had happened and was hell-bent on punishing her!

She paused in the act of pushing the kitchen door open with her foot, her brow wrinkling. Was his conceit so great that he couldn't bear the idea of a mere woman—any woman—giving him the brush-off, even if he'd already found her replacement?

Or could there possibly be an innocent explanation for the way he and the glorious creature he'd been with had been behaving?

Unconsciously, she shook her head. She'd seen what she'd seen, hadn't she? Of course, with hindsight, knowing who he really was altered the scenario. He'd had no need to prey on wealthy women for what he hoped to get out of them financially.

It was a mess. Her head was a mess. She couldn't think straight!

A nudge of the door and she was through. Her breath caught in her throat and stuck there. He was sprawled out on the chair with the broken springs, his eyes closed. He looked so beautiful and strangely, heart-stoppingly vulnerable. In that moment it all came flooding back. All the depth of love she'd once felt for him. Still felt for him?

The fine hairs on the back of her neck prickled as her heart swelled inside her breast, a bitter-sweet pain that took her breath away. And then, as if her involuntary gasp had alerted him, his eyes snapped open. In that unguarded moment, as their eyes met, soul to soul, she stopped fighting the inevitable and said, a shake in her voice, 'I'll do what you want me to do,' because she finally knew she couldn't bear to turn her back on him, lose him, not again.

His eyes on the sudden flush of colour on her face, Diego snapped to his feet. A shock of something hot and insistent raced through his taut body. He had her! Had he ever doubted it? Hadn't he known that the lazy, avaricious minx would always take what she would see as the easy option?

The only acknowledgement he dared allow himself was a brief dip of his dark head. Reaching in an inner pocket, he produced a card and wrote rapidly on the back. 'My mobile number. The address of my hotel. Be there tomorrow evening at eight. We will discuss our itinerary over dinner.'

Insouciantly, he dropped the oblong of pasteboard down on the coffee tray she'd prepared and turned away, reminding himself fiercely that he was no longer the eager besotted fool he'd once been, firmly battening down the primal instinct to take her in his arms and claim some of what he was owed. Feel the sweetness of her lips beneath his own, feel the heated response of her beautiful body. That could wait. No need to display the eagerness that would give her power over him.

Watching him walk to the door, Lisa's eyes were pinned on his wide shoulders and the back of his gleaming dark, proudly held head. She wanted to call him back, tell him she loved him—she'd believed she'd stopped, but she now knew she hadn't—and explain exactly why she'd acted as she had all those years ago.

But his arrogance, his hardness, his curt, almost disdainful acceptance of her submission stopped her. As far as he was concerned this was his due, a hard man's revenge. He would view any protestations of love with cynical distaste.

As the door closed behind him she stuffed her fist between her teeth and felt the tears course hotly down her face.

Leaving the normal Monday morning editorial meeting, Lisa was waylaid by her father's secretary. 'He wants you in his office. Now. And don't worry.' She grinned, seeing the younger woman's distraught expression. 'He's actually in a really good mood today!'

It wasn't her father's mood that was worrying her, Lisa thought distractedly as she walked to his office. It was everything else!

Telling Sophie yesterday of the broken engagement had been a nightmare. Sure, she'd dressed it up as best she could, explaining that having seen Diego again she'd realised she still had feelings for him and marrying Ben wouldn't be fair or right. She'd skipped the blackmail bit simply because since talking to Ben she'd understood that saving the magazine was not what this was about; it was irrelevant.

And since Diego had walked out she'd been having second thoughts. Throughout the day she'd stared at his mobile number until the figures had danced and blurred in front of her eyes, trying to decide whether to phone him and tell him she'd changed her mind.

If he'd shown some emotion, smiled at her even, then she might be feeling differently. Had he taken her hands as he always had done in the past when they'd met, brushing his warm lips slowly over her knuckles before turning them over and placing a lingering kiss in each palm, she would have been ecstatic.

When she'd changed her mind and agreed to what he'd asked she'd felt that they'd only need to touch each other for all the old magic to swamp them both again. But he hadn't touched her and she'd been a real fool to think they could go back to the way it had been because none of it had been real.

So, as it was, she felt insulted. And stupid.

His mobile number was printed indelibly on her mind. She would phone the moment she returned to her office and, hopefully, disguise the hurt in her voice when she told him she'd changed her mind.

Her father was staring at the view from his window. He turned when she entered, a rare smile on his craggy face as he announced, 'You might as well clear your desk today. Under the circumstances there's no need for you to work out your notice. Raffacani has everything in hand.'

Already! 'You've spoken to him?' Lisa felt for the back of one of the chairs that fronted his massive desk.

'He's only just left. He demanded an emergency executive meeting first thing this morning.' His tone was admiring. 'Not one to let the grass grow under his feet. I like that; it augurs well.'

For whom? Lisa asked herself sinkingly as she sat and watched her father take his seat behind the desk, his cold eyes scanning her pale features as if seeing her, really seeing her, for the first time. 'I had no idea you knew each other. Raffacani explained everything. How the two of you met in Spain, how he lost sight of you, and your agreement to spend some time with him in Andalusia.'

He permitted himself another slight smile. 'Play your cards right, convince him you'd make the perfect wife, and you'll be set for life. Mind you, Arthur was cut up. Ben's had his nose knocked out of place—yours was probably the shortest engagement on record. But, as Raffacani's package includes heavy investment, restaffing at the higher editorial levels, he soon came round.' He gave her a judicious look. 'I imagine his rescue package is down to you. I don't want to know the ins and outs of it but I can tell you this—you've actually made up for not being the son I always wanted. Good girl!'

So she had finally won his approval! Lisa swallowed the threatened tears. But at what price? No use telling herself it didn't matter, that she had learned to live with his indifference. All her life she'd wanted his warmth, his approval, his recognition that, despite not being a son, she was flesh of his flesh, his child. It was a need she couldn't shake off in the time it took to take a breath. And to give him his due, she rationalised, he didn't know the true story.

The phone call to Diego wouldn't be made. Couldn't be made, not now. He'd withdraw his rescue package. Her father would blame her. He would hate her!

The little black dress was earning its keep again tonight, was Lisa's self-admittedly ridiculous thought as she paid the taxi off and entered the foyer of one of London's most exclusive hotels.

Anything to stop herself thinking of the humiliation that lay ahead.

She'd showered and dressed like an automaton, coiling her hair up on the back of her head and fixing seed pearl ear studs into her lobes. Sparing with her make-up, she surveyed the finished result with the bleak satisfaction of knowing she looked cool, remote and untouchable. Her Ice Maiden Look, Sophie would have joked if she hadn't still been too miffed with her to speak to her at all.

'I've always thought of you as my kid sister!' Sophie had muttered at her yesterday. 'And my best friend—and it was going to be lovely having you really in the family. And don't forget, it was me who brought Ben up to scratch. I told him to propose to you to keep us all a nice cosy family!'

Lisa hadn't known that. But it made sense. Ben would have thought long and hard about what his twin had suggested and come down on the side of expediency.

He hadn't a romantic or adventurous bone in his body and if he wanted to marry at some stage, start a family, it might as well be with his father's partner's daughter. They were very fond of each other, always had been, knew each other inside out. And after the regrettable interlude with the Spanish waiter she had never put a foot wrong, never even dated. What could be better?

She sighed deeply. She knew the way his mind

worked and could furnish the internal conversation he would have had with himself.

And now she had lost Sophie, her best friend, and Ben too. The three of them would never be as close again. And when Diego had finished with her, tossed her aside like a used tea bag, she would have nothing and no one.

No pride, no self-respect. No job. And all because she had suffered a moment of sheer madness, thinking she and Diego could recapture what they had once had. His attitude as he'd acknowledged her submission had brought her back to sanity.

His room number in her possession, she took one of the lifts. Stiffening her spine, she drew in a deep breath as it stopped at the floor she wanted. She would match his mood, beat for beat. If he could be hard and disdainful, then so could she, curt to the point of rudeness, too, if that was the way he was going to play it. Keeping emotional distance was her only self-defence. Second time around a broken heart would be impossible to mend.

His great wealth had bought him the power to wreak vengeance but that didn't mean he had to gain any kind of satisfaction from it. If he wanted her to have sex with him—making love didn't come near to describing what this sordid bargain was all about—then she would keep her side of the hellish agreement. But he wouldn't enjoy having sex with a lump of wooden indifference.

That would be her revenge!

CHAPTER FIVE

LISA was oblivious of the sheer opulence of Diego's hotel suite; she didn't move more than a foot inside the door he'd opened to her hesitant rap. She didn't smile and she certainly couldn't speak.

She didn't look at him and kept her eyes on the patch of the soft cream carpet directly in front of her feet. But she was so stingingly aware of him her head was swimming, her heart banging wildly against her breastbone. She kept her teeth clamped tightly together. If she relaxed the iron grip they would start chattering with nervous tension.

Was he expecting her to go to bed with him tonight? That would be her side of the bargain, wouldn't it? Her stomach jaunted off on a roller coaster ride of its own at that thought and she emitted a low driven groan.

'Don't slouch.' The lightly accented drawled injunction dragged her back to her senses. She was supposed to be giving him the same cold treatment he'd given her, wasn't she? Not acting like a cringing victim waiting for the axe to fall.

She raised her head slowly, injecting ice into her inky-blue eyes. It was a real struggle to maintain a haughty, indifferent expression when looking into that lean, darkly handsome face and admitted to herself that he would only have to say one kind word to have her melting like a snowflake on hot coals.

Inching her chin higher as the cool narrowed assessment of his beautiful eyes made her pulses jump, she ignored the butterflies in her stomach and drawled as flatly as she could manage, 'Father tells me you've already got your side of the bargain moving.' A slight, resigned shrug. Could she come across as sophisticated and blasé? She had no idea. But she'd give it a try.

'We may as well get my side of it over, too.'

That less than enthusiastic statement should let him know she'd put their arrangement firmly into the boring business category, emotions totally absent.

'If that's an invitation I'm not overwhelmed with joy.' His handsome mouth hardened. *Por Dios*, but she was as hard as nails! But he had expected that, hadn't he? She didn't turn a hair at the idea of using sex as a bargaining tool. Five years ago he'd fallen fathoms deep in love with a sweetly generous, innocent angel. What an act she'd put on!

She was still as lovely, though. Perhaps even more so. Her eyes could still make his soul shake, his body sting with desire. And he would have her, but on his terms, not hers. He would make her beg…

Taking a pace back, he made a small gesture to a table set in front of an enormous window that gave a glittering view of the vibrant, brilliantly lit city. 'I would prefer our relationship to be civilised, so we start as we mean to go on,' he imparted levelly. 'To that end, dinner is already ordered and while we eat we will discuss our future arrangements.'

Ending that cool statement of intent, Diego placed a hand lightly on the small of her back and encouraged her in the direction of the elegantly laid table as the trolley from Room Service arrived, dexterously handled by an impassive-faced waiter.

Lisa was wearing the dress she had worn to the charity function, he recognised. Sexy. Silk. An understated design that hinted tantalisingly at the delicate curves and intriguing hollows of her divine body. He could feel the warmth of her under his palm, the way the silk slid against her body as she moved, and his groin ached fiercely. Had they been alone he would have dragged her into his arms…

And spoiled his plan to make her be the one to beg, go down on her knees and beg until she had no breath left and then, and only then…

The moral was, don't touch. Not yet. Removing his hand smartly, he stepped ahead and held out a chair for her and took his seat opposite, furious that his control over his libido was worse than shaky where she was concerned.

Watching, as stony-faced as she could get considering how his touch had affected her, Lisa envied his urbanity as he approved the wine he had ordered to go with whatever it was the waiter had put on her plate. Diego was clothed in a pale grey suit that shouted class, a white shirt with faint pale grey stripes that accentuated the dusky olive tones of his skin and the permanent five o'clock shadow that had always made her want to run her fingers over the firm set of his jaw.

Still did! Lifting her fork as the waiter withdrew

from the suite—she wasn't remotely hungry but pushing the no doubt delicious food around gave her something to do—she challenged, 'I believe you want to discuss my temporary status as your mistress.' And hoped the business-like tone made him feel as wanted and desirable as a giant black slug in a plate of salad.

But the only effect was a vague upward drift of one slanting black brow, a dismissive, 'The status of mistress is way above what I have in mind for you.' He lifted his wine glass. 'Can I take it that you have a current passport?'

That put-down cut her up. He really did despise her, didn't he? But her voice was sharp as broken glass as she answered his question. 'Of course. Why?'

'We leave for one of my homes in Spain at the end of the week. In the meantime I'll be tied up with lawyers and the ins and outs of putting my man in place to drag *Lifestyle* into the twenty-first century. We won't meet again until early on Friday morning when I pick you up on my way to the airport.'

Lisa shouldn't be poleaxed by that announcement but she was. During that morning's interview with her father she'd been so taken aback by the speed of Diego's movements, the way he'd spiked her guns when it came to changing her mind because she couldn't bear to lose what she'd never had before—her father's approval—she hadn't absorbed the import of his '...your agreement to spend some time with him in Andalusia'. The fact that he'd told her to clear her desk hadn't cut much ice, either. If clued-up editors were to be brought in no one would want her around because she'd be like a fish out of water.

Now her stomach performed one of the spectacular lurches that were becoming all too frequent since coming into contact with Diego Raffacani again. Here in chilly, early spring London she could maintain an indifferent façade. Just. And with supreme difficulty. But back in Spain with him, where it had all started, she wouldn't be able to survive the bitter-sweet pain of it.

Laying down her fork, her eyes clashed with his. It took only a moment to subdue her twanging vocal cords and remark tautly, 'Correct me if I'm wrong, but you said nothing to me about my going to Spain. I thought—'

'Thought a couple of quickies while I'm here in England would pay off the debt,' Diego interrupted drily, his long fingers tightening around the delicate stem of his wine glass. 'Not so. When you recompense me for the way you behaved five years ago it will be at a place and time of my choosing.'

And the little minx wouldn't be acting as though making love with him was a mundane and necessary task like sorting the washing. She would be as willing and eager as she had been five years ago, her sweet lips gasping for the fulfilment he had withheld out of genuine love for her. And when she was on the point of disintegrating he would take her, burn the frustration and anger that had been his private demon for far too long right out of his system. And dump her. Let her know for once what rejection really felt like.

Noting the sudden dark colour that stained his slashing cheekbones, the dark glitter of his eyes beneath the thick fringe of lashes, Lisa tried to block the images of her being used as a cheap sex toy right out of her mind and decided that the time had come to put the record straight. Then, surely, he would reconsider? And let her go. Maybe with an apology and a contrite promise not to withdraw his offer of investment in the magazine.

But did she really want that? the part of her she privately despised commented edgily. Didn't she still hunger for him, despite pretending the opposite? Didn't some perverse and childish hope prod her into fantasising about him falling in love with her? Really falling in love this time, not whiling his spare time away with a silly little teenager, telling her what he thought she wanted to hear because it amused him to see her fall headlong under his spell. Not meaning a single word of it because he spent his evenings, not working as he'd said, but making whoopee with a gorgeous, sophisticated female from his own exalted class who really knew how to please her man.

No, she owed it to herself to wriggle out of his wicked bargain if she possibly could. Owed it to what was left of her self-control and dignity, she vowed, fervently hoping she believed herself. Clutching the bowl of her so far ignored wine glass, she questioned, 'Don't you think we should talk about it?'

The slight upwards drift of one dark brow was the only expression on that lean and dangerously handsome face. 'I believe we have been.'

'No, not that. Not the terms and conditions,' she dismissed thickly, horribly conscious of the hot colour creeping over her skin as the reminder of exactly what he expected of her jumped into her mind with the force of a nuclear explosion. 'But why you're still so angry with me over what happened that night all those years ago. It's a long time to bear a grudge, Diego.' She spoke softly, willing him to listen, to at least understand that the blame wasn't hers entirely. 'I know I acted like a total idiot, but—'

'*Basta!* I have no wish to listen to the tissue of lies you've had time to dream up!' Black eyes glittered with savage contempt. 'You may look like an angel but you lie like the devil!' he informed her with deadly intensity. 'I saw what I saw, I heard what I heard—*perdición*!' He got to his feet, pushing back his chair, looming over her.

Lisa flinched, cut to the heart that he should hate her quite that much. Her eyes swam with unwanted tears as he reminded more levelly, 'The past is a distant country. Forget it. Concentrate on the future, on paying your dues, and, when that is done, it too can be forgotten.'

And she would be forgotten. Just like that! Lisa, too, sprang to her feet. He was cruel. Hard. And the hope that their relationship could develop into a mirror image of what it had been bit the dust. How could she have been so stupid to have fantasised that it might? He had changed out of all recognition.

Facing him, her inky eyes swimming as they collided with his, she acknowledged that he might not have changed at all. Had he always been this callous? The loving front of five years ago just that. A front, assumed for his own careless amusement?

'I hate you!' she spat with driven vehemence.

'Ah! That is good.' A slow, deliberate stride

brought him round the table to her quivering side, the slightest of smiles curving a mouth that was far too kissable for her own good. Two strong and almost painfully gentle hands cupped her face, setting up a chain reaction that made her tremble with far more than outraged anger and deep hurt. 'Any strong emotion is preferable to indifference, is it not?' Then he did what she'd been secretly hoping and dreading in equal measure.

He kissed her.

The effect of that wide sensual mouth on hers set off a volcanic explosion deep inside her, pulsing the ripples of aftershock right through every nerve and vein in her body. Had her matching his hungry urgency with a driven desperation that shattered her into launching herself against his powerful frame, looping her arms around his neck, her avid fingers tangling in the soft midnight darkness of his hair.

He tasted of hot male passion and she couldn't get enough of him. He was all she'd ever wanted, the only man she'd ever loved. Her body melted into him, her breasts peaking with open invitation, her lips matching his ravaging assault.

Her lips were still tingling, her knees shamefully shaky, when a short time later Diego handed her into the taxi he'd summoned to take her home. Her mind was still sickened by the ease with which he'd held her away from him when her response had threatened to get way out of hand. His coolly delivered, almost uninvolved comment that it was time she went home and a reminder that he'd call for her on Friday morning around seven-thirty was still ringing in ears that burned with shame. All capped off with the flatly delivered threat that he'd find her if she should be misguided enough to flee. It was a timely reminder of the humiliation he would dole out if she ever again was unguarded enough to demonstrate how she hungered for him.

An hour later she fell into bed still in a state of deep shock. Mostly induced by what her own behaviour had revealed about her. Diego Raffacani was a cruel blackmailing louse. So arrogantly sure of himself that he out and out refused to listen to a word she had to say in her own defence. He'd called her a liar and that alone should have put her off him for several lifetimes. But no, oh no! What had she gone and done? Shown him how needy she was, eager and straining against him, possessed by a frantic hunger for him.

She was still in love with him. She sobbed into her pillow. He was the only man she had ever loved. Far from being the promiscuous tramp of his imagining, she was still a virgin. Ben, the only other man she'd ever been involved with, had never inspired this wild yearning.

There had to be something drastically wrong with her if she could be in love with a man who was entirely without scruples or conscience. A man who intended to take her to his bed as an act of revenge, who had convinced himself that the blame for the way she'd insulted his precious pride, when she'd been too young to realise what she was doing, was hers entirely.

The immediate future looked bleaker than the lunar landscape. Lisa had no idea how she would survive it.

His car, a low sporty model, was waiting at the airport, delivered there by his Spanish minions, Lisa deduced grumpily, her spiky mood the legacy of a mostly sleepless night as she'd tried and failed to come to terms with what she was letting herself in for, the alarm clock ringing spitefully just as she had been finally dropping off. Her mood was not lightened by the sight of Diego arriving precisely at seven-thirty.

'Ready?' he enquired briskly, looking as if he'd had the benefit of a full eight hours sleep, a revitalising shower and a hearty breakfast.

'I haven't finished packing.' A lie. She hadn't started. Ever since that evening at his hotel suite she'd been hoping that something would happen to make him call this whole thing off. But he hadn't miraculously lost his memory and she hadn't broken a leg!

'Then I suggest you get on with it. The taxi is waiting. If you are always this disorganised I'm amazed that you held down any sort of job at all, even one manufactured by a doting father.'

Her irritation level rose a thousand-fold. What did he know? 'Dad doesn't dote!' she snapped and stamped into her bedroom to drag things out of drawers and cupboards and stuff them into a small suitcase.

Ever since then he'd been irritating the life out of her. Throughout the ride to the airport, the business of checking in and the flight itself he had been coolly polite and dutifully attentive. As if she were a virtual stranger he had found himself dragooned into escorting, when in harsh reality she was the woman he was callously blackmailing into becoming his temporary mistress.

Sub-mistress, she amended on a spurt of irrational anger. Though why she should object to the irrelevant point of being regarded as too low to be afforded even the slightly denigrating title of mistress only went to show what a muddle her mind was in. Whereas he, drat it, was calm and collected, single-minded, determined on one thing only—to take her to his bed and punish her for damaging his precious pride.

And then get rid of her.

Now, with the airport an hour's drive behind them, Diego asked, 'What did you mean when you said your father didn't dote?'

Lisa dragged her eyes from the alarmingly twisty narrow road that snaked up into the mountains and fastened her gaze on his impressively chiselled profile. It was the first personal remark he'd made since they'd entered the waiting taxi back in London.

Shrugging slightly, she returned her attention to the view. Now and then she caught the glitter of the sea and, unlike London, the air cocooned her in welcome warmth. 'I meant precisely what I said.' Her relationship with her father was something she wasn't prepared to discuss and, turning the subject, she asked, 'So where are we going? How much further?'

Diego's shoulders tautened as he handled the tortuous hairpin bends with practised ease. Who the hell did she think she was kidding? She would have been spoiled rotten from birth. What father worth the name wouldn't slavishly lavish all his attention on such an outwardly bewitching little charmer, even more so after she'd been left motherless at a relatively tender age?

A memory from five years ago, as clear as all the myriad others that had haunted him for so long, assaulted him. The day he found he'd lost his watch. She'd held hers out to him. The thing would have cost a small fortune. And when he'd commented she'd simply shrugged. 'My father's birthday gift', as if it were a mere trinket.

The spoiled brat had been given a responsible job on the magazine staff even though the whole enterprise was going pear-shaped and what had been desperately needed was an experienced editor. The fabulous dress she'd been wearing at her engagement party must have cost another small fortune, the wherewithal doubtless supplied by doting daddy.

And that sparked a different train of thought.

'How did Ben take the broken engagement?' He'd noticed the absence of the diamond hoop. He noticed every damn thing about her. He remembered his own desperate pain when the spoiled brat had as good as told him to shove off and wondered, guiltily, if Ben Clayton had felt the same, wondered if his initial thought, that he'd actually been doing the poor sucker a favour, still held water.

'That's not really any of your business, is it?' Lisa dismissed edgily. How could she tell him that hers and Ben's would have been a passionless marriage, based on nothing more exciting than long-standing affection and mutual respect? That Ben had been wise enough to predict that even that kind of marriage couldn't survive if one partner were still in thrall to a long-ago lost love?

'And you haven't answered my question,' she reminded him snappily. 'I have a right to know where you're taking me.'

Fully expecting him to tell her she had no rights at all and to continue prodding about her broken engagement—did the cruel streak in him want to hear that Ben had been devastated, suicidal?—she was stunned when he answered equably, 'To my favourite hideout. It used to be a monastery. The family rarely uses it these days. The area isn't frequented by hordes of tourists; its beauty and tranquillity remain intact. Unlike Marbella,' he added drily. 'You will find no beautiful people, no glitzy shops, fabulous yachts or smart hotels to claim your attention. You will give it all to pleasing me.'

She should have kept her mouth shut, Lisa recognised sickly. Whatever she said he managed to come back with something designed to put her down.

The next days or weeks promised to be a nightmare of humiliation and pain, she acknowledged, the hauntingly beautiful landscape lost in a sudden blur of stingingly hot tears.

CHAPTER SIX

LISA couldn't fault the beauty and comfort of Diego's preferred hideout. Built centuries ago of mellow golden stone, the former monastery commanded an impressive view over fertile valleys, thickly wooded slopes and tantalising glimpses of the sparkling blue sea between towering mountain crags.

She couldn't fault Diego's behaviour, either, she told herself edgily as she paced the flagged stone terrace in the soft dawn light.

She almost wished she could.

She would have better understood where he was coming from if he'd done as she had expected and taken her to his bed that first night. She might not have liked it—she might have liked it far too much, she corrected with painful honesty as her restless feet brought her to the end of the terrace—but at least she would have understood it.

What she was at a loss to puzzle out was why she'd been given her own suite of rooms. Beautiful, restful rooms that he had shown no inclination to visit. Why, during her nearly four whole days here now, he'd done nothing more alarming than treat her as a house guest. He had joined her for meals, during which his conversation had entranced her against her will—witty, perceptive and at times, hardest of all to bear, cool and painfully impersonal. And all the while he had seemed to look straight through her, not really seeing her at all.

Between meals he'd taken himself off to his study, explaining courteously that he had much work to get through, leaving her to her own devices. Her own thoughts.

Her hands tightened on the warm stone of the balustrade. She knew what he had planned for her, what she was expected to be. So what was he waiting for? Why was he behaving like a great jungle cat, stalking a prey he was not yet hungry for yet never really letting it out of his sight?

Her whole body was tingling with sexual tension, her mind edgy, her nerve-ends as jumpy as a flea on a griddle.

'Quite the early bird. Couldn't you sleep?'

The unexpected soft laid-back drawl made the hairs on the back of her neck stand to attention, made her heart leap to her throat and jump about like a frightened trapped animal.

Lean hands on her shoulders turned her to face him. As always he looked spectacular, she noted with feverish tension. Dressed this morning in stone-coloured chinos with an olive-green lawn shirt tucked into his narrow waistline, his shatteringly masculine features were bland, but instead of looking through her as usual his sultry black-fringed eyes were making a slow, devastating inventory of her quivering frame.

This close he was dynamite, always had been. Lisa tried to smother an inrush of sobbing breath as she felt the betrayal of her peaking breasts beneath the checked flannelette shirt she was wearing over an old pair of jeans. His eyes on her body felt like a physical caress. A caress he was denying her.

Because he'd changed his mind and he no longer wanted to touch her?

A hand lifted from her shoulder in answer to the unspoken question that glittered in her eyes, long tanned fingers brushing the fall of her hair away from her face. The backs of his fingers lingered slightly, seductively, scorching her skin.

She was hot all over, so hot, burning up, fiery heat pooling between her thighs, making her legs shake. She was trying to make her face as expressionless as a lump of stone but, in spite of the effort she was making, could he guess what he did to her? He slowly dropped both hands and remarked lightly, 'Breakfast awaits. Pilar saw you were up and about and thought we might prefer to eat in the courtyard. Come.'

Her unfortunately mesmerised eyes on the length of his legs, on his seemingly indolent stride as he led the way, Lisa felt on the point of collapse when she took her seat in the central courtyard, shaded at this time of the morning from the rapidly increasing heat of the sun.

White doves called sleepily from the trees that overhung the high stone walls and the scent of a myriad flowers perfumed the air. In any other circumstances she would have revelled in this much perfection.

Ever the attentive host, Diego poured juice for her and passed her the fruit bowl. Lisa, selecting a peach she had no appetite for, tried not to scream.

If today were to follow the pattern of all the others

since she'd been here he would make light conversation while they ate, suggest a walk she might like to take before the real heat of the day, and then excuse himself politely and spend his time shut away in his study.

And she would play the part she had assigned herself, give a bored, dismissive shrug, as if she couldn't care less, and wonder how long she could keep up the act of total indifference.

Asking why he was spending as little time as possible with her was quite out of the question. It would let him know she was hankering for his attention. Desperate for it, even. His twenty-four-hour-a-day intimate attention! It was the reason he'd brought her here in the first place, wasn't it? she thought wildly to excuse her shameless longing to be held in his arms, to have his mouth create havoc with hers, to…

'We'll drive down into Marbella this morning,' Diego imparted as he laid his napkin down. 'You appear to have packed nothing but heavy jeans and shirts.' A censorious glance at the perspiring pallor of her overheated face. 'Suitable for doing the weekend chores in chilly London but not for this climate, this ambience.' He poured them both a second cup of coffee as he stated, 'I'll buy you the right clothes.'

Too dazed by his intention to spend time with her just when she'd been agonising over his four day long disinclination to do any such thing to say a word, Lisa struggled to think of a single thing to say.

Was this the beginning?

Her heart began to race, her breathing going haywire, colour flooding her face. Obviously, the workaday stuff she'd shoved so carelessly into her suitcase wasn't turning him on. What did he have in mind? Pelmet-sized mini-skirts, black fishnet stockings, six-inch heels and minute crop tops decorated with purple sequins?

Hadn't he as good as said he'd treat her like a hooker, the title of temporary mistress being far too good for her in his haughty opinion? Was he expecting her to dress like one too?

The idea was so absurd she didn't know whether to laugh or to cry, just stared at him instead, her pale cheeks blooming with pink, aware that her mouth had dropped open but unable to do anything about it.

Replacing his coffee cup on its saucer with a clatter, Diego got to his feet, noting her wide-eyed, open-mouthed look of pleasure with grim distaste.

Greed.

It was the first genuine emotion she'd displayed since they'd arrived here. She'd looked edgy or bored during their carefully rationed meetings. He'd only had to mention buying her a few new outfits to have her lighting up like a Christmas tree. But what else had he expected? he asked himself tersely before telling her flatly, 'Manuel's bringing the car round. I'll see you on the forecourt in ten minutes.'

Ten minutes to get her racing heartbeat back to normal, to calm herself sufficiently to face what appeared to be the next stage of the game.

Because he was playing games, she told herself agitatedly as she exchanged the checked shirt for a marginally more attractive ribbed cotton sweater in a shade of deep raspberry pink and hurriedly applied a toning lipstick. What else could explain the way he'd left her largely to her own devices, never once mentioning the real reason for her being here, much less acting on it?

Today he intended to spend time with her. Today he'd touched her, his hands on her shoulders, his fingers brushing the skin of her cheek as he'd pushed her hair back from her face. The second stage of the game was obviously about to begin.

Which didn't do her pulse rate any good at all, she recognised as she scraped her hair back in a ponytail, acknowledging that she, too, was playing games. Affecting indifference, boredom even, was all very well but she had the sinking feeling that she wouldn't be able to keep it up for much longer because he was turning out to be a real expert when it came to winding her up.

A fact amply demonstrated by the easy way he talked to her as he drove, giving her a potted history of the former monastery, explaining that his grandfather had bought it many years ago, had it restored by experts and turned into a tasteful home without losing any of the atmosphere. 'But my parents rarely use it; they find it far too isolated. If I didn't love it, come here whenever I can, keep on a skeleton staff, it would fall back into dereliction.'

As he talked his features softened, coming to vibrant life. Lisa swallowed thickly, averting her eyes from the intimate warmth of the sideways glittering glance he bestowed on her.

This was Diego as she remembered him. The Diego she had fallen in love with. Charming, vital, fascinating. And dangerous, she reminded herself on a tingling *frisson* of unstoppable sexual excitement.

The narrow road was descending through a thick belt of woodland, the air just slightly cooler, which hopefully went some way towards excusing the shiver that racketed through her.

'Scared?' he asked softly, his eyes knowing as he glanced at her, his long mouth curving with what looked suspiciously like male satisfaction as he gave his concentration back to the twisting tarmac.

Lisa knew what he was talking about. But no way would she admit to being affected in any way at all by his far more intimate, softer attitude. 'Not at all,' she murmured drily. 'You drive well, so why should I be scared? Just chilly, that's all.'

His open grin told her he didn't believe a word of it. Even beneath the trees the cooler air was still soft and warm. No one could possibly feel chilly!

'But of course,' he murmured tauntingly. 'What else could make you shudder to the soles of your pretty little feet?'

It was time she straightened things out between them, put a stop to this cat and mouse game of his, Lisa fulminated inwardly. Against all common sense she might still secretly and hopelessly love the wretch but she hated the way he seemed to be manipulating her.

As they approached the outskirts of the coastal playground of the seriously wealthy she told him, 'I wasn't thinking straight when I packed. I'd forgotten the huge difference in climate, even at this time of year. My fault,' she admitted stiffly, wishing she hadn't been in such a contrary, ill-tempered mood when she'd thrown just any old thing into her suitcase. 'And I'll buy my own clothes, thanks all the same.'

A couple of cotton skirts and tops would be as much as she could afford. Marbella wasn't the place to come if you were shopping on a budget, she decided wryly, thinking of her tiny bank balance and the fact that she had no job to go back to.

'I wouldn't hear of it,' Diego stated firmly as he found a parking spot. Turning to her, he slid an arm along the back of her seat, deft fingers finding the narrow ribbon that pulled her hair starkly back off her face and removing it. His voice was now a soft velvet purr, making her tremble. 'At the risk of sounding incredibly vulgar, I can afford it. Particularly as the doting daddy isn't with us to pick up your bills.'

'Don't!' Lisa snapped, hot colour flooding her cheeks. The ribbon was disappearing into his trouser pockets; to try to take it back would result in an unseemly tussle which she, of course, would lose. And she'd had more than enough of his mind games. 'If you mention my supposedly doting father one more time I'll—I'll hit you!'

Hard fingers fastened around her wrist as she attempted to scramble out of the car, pulling her back to face him. One ebony brow arched as he murmured, 'Hit me and I'll retaliate.' His eyes dropped to the kissable, trembling pout of her mouth and lingered there. 'But not with physical violence. There are other, pleasanter ways of subduing a woman.'

A stab of satisfaction forked its lightning way

through his body. He'd left her to stew for four whole days and nights, keeping her on an emotional knife-edge. Her veneer of indifference was cracking up and he was going to make it crumble to dust.

A slow smile curved his mouth as his words brought the frost back into those huge inky-blue eyes, her lips tightening in mute rebuttal. She was fighting her corner with every atom of her will-power but before too long he would have her as weak as a kitten, begging him to end the impasse, clinging to him, her body on fire for him and only him.

As his loins tightened Diego wiped out that train of thought and slowly released her wrist, frowning at the band of reddened skin. 'A long cold drink's in order before we hit the shops.'

And he would foot the bill for clothes that would be more comfortable and do justice to her ethereal loveliness, in spite of her unexpected refusal to let him. A refusal that was surely just lip-service to the conventions? Easily forgotten in the face of the slightest pressure?

Pondering that, he joined her on the pavement. She was wearing the strap of her shoulder bag across her body. It lay diagonally between the pert perfectly shaped breasts that were lovingly shaped by the softly clinging pink cotton of the top she'd changed into. The worn denim of her jeans moulded the curve of her hips, the rounded temptation of her thighs.

He snapped his eyes away. *Cristo!* She was pure temptation. Before he knew it he would be the one down on his knees and begging! That was not part of his plan. She, not he, would abase herself, plead with him—not the other way round!

Fifty yards brought them to the nearest pavement café. He led her to a table shaded by an arbour of vines with a panoramic view of the glittering blue sea. Ordering Buck's Fizz for Lisa and plain orange juice for himself, Diego allowed the atmosphere between them to settle before probing something that was beginning to puzzle him.

'Tell me something, Lisa,' he murmured when he noted the signs of the beginnings of relaxation in the easing of her tense shoulders, the way her fingers now lay loosely around her thirstily emptied glass. 'Why do you get so angry whenever I combine the words daddy and doting in the same sentence?'

'Because you don't know what you're talking about,' Lisa came back without heat. That drink had been delicious, dissolving her annoyance, bringing the ghost of a smile at the thought that anyone could imagine that Gerald Pennington had fond fatherly feelings for his small, insignificant daughter.

'Then why don't you enlighten me?' A click of his lean fingers brought a waiter with a fresh glass of Buck's Fizz to the table. Diego watched the look of surprise and pleasure cross her lovely face and waited until she'd taken the first appreciative sip before pressing softly, 'I like to know what I'm talking about. It gives me more—' he paused a moment before adding with self-mocking solemnity '—more *gravitas*.'

Her brilliant eyes swept up to lock with his and she giggled softly, just as he'd intended. Diego felt a pang of self-dislike as he remembered that she'd eaten nothing for breakfast, merely mangling the peach she'd taken. Then brushed it aside. He wasn't aiming to get her drunk, just relaxed enough to rid her of that slightly edgy indifference.

'Well—' Her slim shoulders lifted in a careless shrug. She took one more sip then decided to leave the rest. She was beginning to feel light-headed and that wasn't a good idea around Diego Raffacani. She needed all her wits about her.

Pulling in a tight breath, she told him, 'My father showed little interest in me while my mother was alive and even less after her death. When I was home from boarding school I was farmed out on to his partner's family—that's why I'm so close to Sophie and Ben.'

Lisa sucked her lower lip between her teeth, her eyes clouding with regret. Had been close, she mentally amended. Not any more.

Seeing her sudden distress, Diego frowned. His instinct was to take the small slender hands that were lying on the top of the table and enfold them with his. He denied it with difficulty.

'Maybe he was grief-stricken after your mother's tragically early death, but wanted you to be able to move on,' he suggested even-handedly, trying to understand why a man with a needy, fragile girl-child could farm her out to someone else. Where he came from people looked after their own. Family was of the first importance.

Lisa pulled a derisory face. 'You obviously don't know my father!'

Fishing for sympathy, the stock-in-trade of a spoiled brat?

Diego stated softly, 'Maybe not. But I do know he gave you expensive gifts and eventually, probably because he could think of nothing else to do with you, put you in a responsible position on *Lifestyle*. Did you get your degree, by the way?'

The illusory mists of his seemingly gentle interest cleared from Lisa's eyes. If that wasn't scorn in his deep voice then she was a monkey's uncle!

'The only thing he ever gave me was a book token each Christmas—and a watch for my eighteenth, and he didn't even choose it himself; Honor Clayton let slip that he'd asked her to pick something out. And, as for getting my degree—I didn't get the chance, did I?' she shot back at him. 'As soon as I got back from Spain he told me the publishing empire had shrunk to the size of a small island—*Lifestyle*! He asked me—more or less commanded, now I come to think of it—to give up my university place and join the staff, dogsbodying, trying to learn the ropes. All hands on deck and everyone pulling together is the phrase I remember.'

'And you were happy with that sacrifice?' Diego wanted to know, a slight frown pulling his slanting ebony brows together.

Her mouth set stubbornly. 'No. Just flattered that for once he was noticing me, wanting something. Of course I agreed. I wanted to please him, didn't I? I wanted him to value me.'

Diego felt his breath lock in his lungs. Her lovely eyes had flooded with moisture. His own eyes narrowed as he watched her blink furiously, drag in a breath and essay a tight smile as if to signify she'd said too much, revealed too much.

'Shall we go?' As she began to get to her feet, Diego captured both of her hands and held her.

'In a moment.'

Her hands felt so small within his. The delicacy of her bone structure had aroused all his protective instincts five years ago, left him in awe of her fragile beauty. As his eyes narrowed on the exquisitely modelled features, the soft mouth that trembled slightly, he could feel it happening all over again. The need to cherish and adore.

If she was telling the truth about her relationship with her father, and he was pretty sure she was, then he had misjudged her, he acknowledged heavily.

Had he misjudged her in other ways? Should he listen to what she had to say about that dreadful night without cynically presuming that whatever she said would be a tissue of lies?

If he confessed what his conscience was belatedly telling him—that he'd been wrong to give her no option but to break her engagement, come to Spain with him—then maybe, just maybe, they could start all over again. The spark was still there; it had been playing havoc with him since meeting up with her again. And they were both older and wiser.

Then the small, passive hands came to life, the slender fingers curving around his, and the effect was electrifying.

He said thickly, 'And did he? Value you?'

Lisa couldn't answer. Simply stared into his lean,

dark, shatteringly gorgeous face. Holding Diego's strong warm hands knocked all the breath from her body, made her quiver with a thousand memories of how it had been for them in those far off days when she'd truly believed he'd loved her as passionately as she'd loved him. She wanted to be back in that beautiful magical time with a fierce longing that pushed everything else right out of her head.

She gently withdrew her hands from his and felt the loss of physical contact like a pain. She tried to concentrate on what he'd been asking her.

'He gave no sign of it,' she said at last, sadness darkening her eyes.

Diego leaned over the table, the dark glitter of his eyes pinning her to the spot. 'What kind of man is he?' he asked rawly.

'I honestly don't know,' she answered truthfully. 'He never let me close enough to find out.'

'Yet you agreed to my demands, broke your engagement and, presumably, hurt the man you were supposed to be in love with, just to save the business and future financial security of a man who, from your account, showed very little parental interest in you.'

Put like that, so baldly, didn't explain her lifelong need to earn her father's approval and once having got it how she hadn't wanted to let it go.

Lisa shook her suddenly aching head. She wished she hadn't emptied that first glass so rapidly, wished she hadn't started this. 'It wasn't quite like that. You make me sound really hard-hearted. Ben and I never loved each other.'

Automatically, she glanced down at her ringless

finger. 'We've always been fond of each other and I suppose we just drifted into the idea of marriage.' A tiny shrug. 'Actually, it was Ben who convinced me that letting *Lifestyle* fold wouldn't be the end of the world for our parents, or for the staff. That I could tell you where to put your "demands" with an easy conscience.'

But she hadn't, had she? A tide of warmth spread through the entire and towering length of Diego's body as he stood up from the table and held out his hand to her. Which must mean she had come because she wanted to. Which, in turn, meant that she still felt something for him. *Madre de Dios!* If the past could be forgiven, the bitter years erased, then…

'I was on the point of phoning you,' she told him as they reached the sun-drenched pavement and fell in step. 'And telling you I'd changed my mind and the deal was off, when my father told me he'd already had a meeting with you. I don't know what you said to him but he'd got the idea that your rescue package had everything to do with our knowing each other in the past.'

Her mouth curved in a wry smile, aware that her tongue was still running away with her. 'He told me I'd finally made up for not being the son he'd always wanted. Call me a fool if you like—I probably deserve it. But I couldn't tell him the whole thing was off and have him go from being indifferent to me to actively hating me, could I?'

Suddenly, for Diego, the sun went in. His blood ran cold then burned with fire. *Imbécil!* Had he no more sense than he'd had five years ago? Of course she hadn't agreed to come because she still wanted him, cared something for him!

She'd as good as sold herself to him for a period of time to earn her father's approval.

He put his jealousy of the other man—her own father, for pity's sake—down to anger, gritted the hard clean line of his jaw, the bitterness flooding back, and decided to take full advantage of what he'd bought and paid for.

Lisa.

CHAPTER SEVEN

EVERYTHING had changed; she knew it had. The smallest shake of the kaleidoscope and a new pattern emerged. Pausing at the head of the wide stone staircase, wearing the ice-blue chiffon slip dress Diego had picked out for her, Lisa pinned down the defining moment.

It had come when she'd explained exactly why she'd agreed to his blackmail, back in Marbella that morning, when Buck's Fizz rapidly hitting an empty stomach had loosened her tongue.

To an onlooker the change in him might have been too subtle to cause comment. But to her, finely attuned to everything about Diego Raffacani, it had hit her like a ton of bricks.

Autocratic didn't come near to describing the way he'd stalked the pavements as if he owned the whole town and everyone and everything in it. His dark head high, his handsome face wearing the slightly contemptuous, highly assured expression of a man who knew his smallest whim would be immediately and fawningly catered to, he had ushered her through the plate glass doors of a high fashion boutique, the exclusive sort that had made Lisa feel immediately awestruck and very out of place in her worn jeans and bright pink top.

And she had simply, weakly, let it all happen.

Attended by a tall, pin-thin gushing thirty-something with a permanent soulless smile, Diego had lounged back in a silk-covered baroque-style chair while garments of unbelievable style and quality had been paraded for his lordly nod of approval.

Two hours later a fresh faced youth, wearing a formal light grey suit and an aura of his own importance, had carried an armload of classy carriers and boxes to Diego's car. Lisa had thought let him waste his money if he wants to, and almost had hysterics.

After a late lunch during which little was said and even less eaten they had begun the long drive back to the old monastery. Gripped with a strange foreboding, due to the new cold-edged authority she detected in him, the sense that he saw her as a mere puppet, bought and paid for and designed to perform whenever he pulled the strings, she couldn't regret having opened up to him, not only about her relationships with her father and Ben but her reason for agreeing to his demands in the first place.

It had been a release of sorts, she decided as she began the lonely journey down to the main dining hall. And it was high time Diego opened up too. Ever since they'd met up again they had both been skirting around too many secret thoughts. Condemnatory thoughts coming from both directions, she supposed. Whatever, it would be better if they were spoken.

Manuel had carried the mountain of carriers up to her rooms on their return and Diego had broken his silence to tell her, 'Wear something beautiful. Tonight we eat in the formal dining hall and I like my possessions to be easy on the eye.'

His possession!

Earlier today that would have made her shudder; now she was able to take it in her stride. And she'd done as he'd asked, picked out this dress from the dozens of garments that Rosa, Manuel's pretty wife, had taken from the tissue-packed carriers and hung in the walk-in wardrobe.

High heeled court shoes covered in a matching ice-blue silk gave her much needed extra height. She'd brushed her hair until it fell around her shoulders like a pale blonde waterfall, caught back from one side of her face with a tiny jet clip, and gone to town with her make-up.

He couldn't accuse her of being an eyesore, although by the time she'd finished with him he'd probably accuse her of being a pain in the neck. Things couldn't go on as they were. And tonight she was going to make damned sure that they didn't!

Previously they'd taken their meals in the inner courtyard or in the small, homely breakfast room that overlooked the front terraces and the sweeping views of the mountains. If he'd chosen the formality of the great dining hall to humble her he wasn't going to succeed, she vowed as she opened the heavily carved double doors.

It was an impressive room by any standards, the carved vaulted ceiling soaring way above, lit by massive wrought metal chandeliers, the frescoed walls punctuated by narrow arched windows, the immense glossy-as-glass table set with two places, one at either end.

Biting back the flippant comment that they would

need walkie-talkies to converse with each other, Lisa walked forward, high heels tapping out a confident tattoo on the wide polished boards. Diego rose from the carved chair at the head of the table, a glass of what looked like whisky in one hand.

Dressed formally, he all but took her breath away. Elegant, immaculate and as cold as charity.

During his measured approach his heavily veiled eyes made a lengthy assessment, from the silky fall of her hair, over slender shoulders that the narrow straps of her dress left bare, the pert swell of her breasts and down to the slender length of legs made elegantly longer by the just above the knee hemline and spiky heels.

It was difficult not to squirm beneath that expressionless scrutiny but Lisa just about managed it, nearly sagging with relief when he dipped his head, maybe in approval, maybe not, and turned to walk to a plain oak side table set near the hooded hearth where logs burned brightly against the evening chill of this immense stone room. Then she stiffened when he returned with a flat leather-covered box in his hands and told her, 'Not knowing what colour you would choose to wear, I decided diamonds would be the safest selection.'

The diamonds glittered with cold fire from their bed of faded blue velvet. Appalled, Lisa's eyes widened as he lifted the choker of magnificent stones in an elaborate white gold setting and moved behind her to fasten it around her neck.

Her vow to remain steadfastly calm and sensible

flew out of her head as she jerked away and blurted, 'I don't want them!'

'You're not getting them, believe me. They are on loan for this evening only. To complete the picture and give me the pleasure of looking at outward perfection.'

Smarting under that deliberate put down, Lisa stood like a stone when he brushed her hair aside and fastened the choker around her neck. Move by so much as an inch and those strong hands would pull her back to him again. The touch of his hands would start her shaking all over. Already, knowing that those long fingers were just a hair's breadth away from her skin as he dealt with the tricky clasp, a tingling sensation spread all the way through her.

The bracelet came next. A double row of fine stones in an exquisite setting that matched that of the choker. Diego said flatly, 'The family jewels my mother finds too old-fashioned for her tastes are kept in the strong room here. She sometimes picks through them when she and my father visit. She says it gives her something to do.'

Diamond studs with tear-shaped droppers completed the suite. The backs of his fingers brushed the heated skin of her cheeks as he fixed them in place. When he stood back a pace to survey the finished result Lisa, even though her face was flaming as the result of that light, erotic touch, got a little of her own back as she asked with manufactured brightness, 'How often do they visit? Shall I meet them?' knowing that in his present mood of icy dignity the question would affront him.

'Hardly. There are women a man would be happy to introduce to his parents. Patently, you are not one of them,' he replied, a honed edge to his voice, and she knew she'd been right in her assumption and didn't care because, after what she had to say to him tonight, he wouldn't be able to hurt her any more.

At least that was what she told herself as Rosa and Manuel arrived to serve dinner, but when Diego held her chair out for her and murmured softly for her ears only, 'I will have something beautiful to look at while we eat. The sight of you will give me pleasure,' she wasn't so sure. He could hurt her simply by being himself, a man who was loved and loathed in equal and utterly confusing measure. Did she want to give him that kind of pleasure? The cool, objective pleasure of a man who had acquired an expensive artefact. Like the diamonds, a possession to be admired occasionally then locked away again and forgotten. Certainly not the pleasure of passionate possession. And that did hurt although she did her best to convince herself that it shouldn't.

Between them, Rosa and Manuel served the baked scallops, poured wine, brought quails with herb dressing and roast vegetable salad, poured more wine and finally left them with coffee and little dishes of cream-filled profiteroles and tiny baskets of fruit.

'You should kit them out with roller skates,' Lisa said with forced lightness, an attempt to counteract the unnerving effect of having his eyes on her throughout the seemingly interminable meal. 'They'd get from one end of this mile-long table much quicker.' She said it partly to amuse herself but most of all to let him know that all this formal splendour, the king's ransom of diamonds on her neck her arm and in her ears, wasn't impressing her at all.

No reaction. Diego leaned against the elaborately carved back of his chair, his hands lightly placed on the armrests, his eyes still on her, considering. So she said firmly, 'I'm leaving in the morning. Even if I have to walk. Do what you like about the rescue package you put together. This unpleasant charade is beginning to bore me and I've decided that if you pull out of your side of the bargain I can put up with my father's displeasure. After all, I've endured it, or something very like it, for all of my life.'

She hadn't meant it, any of it, had only said it to jolt him out of this new unbearably autocratic coldness. She didn't want to leave until they'd talked over the wrongs of five years ago. He didn't know she'd seen him with that beautiful woman, witnessed so painfully how they'd been together, so he couldn't know her subsequent bad behaviour had been down to a heart that was shattered and twisted with jealousy.

It was time the truth came out. All of it. He'd stopped her, back in London, by saying he wasn't prepared to listen to a 'tissue of lies'. Somehow she had to force him to hear her side of the story.

The sudden unwelcome thought that he might be just as bored by the charade as she'd said she was and would immediately agree to her leaving, chilled her for a moment, but the bleak smile he gave her, the softly spoken, 'If you go, I'll follow. If you hide, I'll find you,' froze her to the very core of her being.

For all the softening of his voice it sounded menacing but she wouldn't let it throw her. She said brittly, 'I'm sure there must be a law against that sort of harassment. And there's no law that says I have to stay here. However—' she took a last sip of her wine to bolster the nonchalant image she was desperate to portray '—I'll stay if you agree to answer one or two questions. But not here—it's far too formal. I'll be in the courtyard if you think you can go along with that.'

How she got out of that room without falling down she would never know. And she didn't know if he would follow, either. But he did, unnumbered, nerve-scratching minutes later.

He had shed the jacket of his dark immaculate suit and the sleeves of his white shirt were rolled up above his elbows, his black tie discarded. In the pale moonlight he dazzled her with his physical perfection, with the careless arrogance of the way he moved.

He had taken his time before joining her but at least he looked far more approachable, Lisa decided thankfully, monitoring the shiver of excited anticipation that quivered down her spine at the thought that at last they could go some way towards sorting out the past, putting it behind them.

But she changed her mind, realising that nothing concerning him could ever be that easy when he walked over the moon-bathed flagstones to the table beneath the sheltering, shading branches of an ancient fig tree and drawled, 'Let's get one thing straight, shall we? You may ask questions but I may not choose to answer them. And you stay here until I say you may go.' He put the bottle and glasses he carried down on the table. 'Sit where I can see you.' He indicated a seat facing the vine-covered wall and miraculously the area was flooded with soft light.

He must have pressed a hidden switch, Lisa thought distractedly as the diffused light of concealed uplighters and downlighters glowed through banks of lush foliage. He was obviously in no mood for a heart-to-heart, no mood for closure.

Diego Raffacani was still pulling her strings, she thought sinkingly as she sat where he had said she must. And, to her shame, she was actually letting him.

Determined to do something about that degrading state of affairs, she sat up very straight and said, 'You're treating me like a criminal. You heap the blame for what happened five years ago entirely on me. But consider this—you lied to me from the first time we met. So what does that make you?'

A liar, she answered inside her head, her eyes lowered as he calmly poured wine into both glasses, pushing one of them across the table to her. And the only man she had ever loved. After him, no other man could hope to hold her stupid heart in the palm of his hand—and she still wanted him, warts and all, she acknowledged unhappily.

She wanted her Diego back, back the way he had been in those ecstatic days when they had been falling in love with each other. But it wasn't going to happen. Not a chance. He had not been what she had thought he was. Now she was seeing him in his true colours. And still wanting him, for her sins!

He lowered himself into the seat opposite hers. That was better because six foot plus of looming, magnificent, sexually charged manhood was more than she felt she could possibly cope with. But it made little difference to the lurching sensation around her heart because, whereas she was illuminated, he was in shadow.

It was impossible to read his expression, make a stab at guessing what he was thinking. His voice was just slightly amused as he came back with, 'As a criminal you're getting five star treatment without receiving your punishment. I really wouldn't complain if I were you. And—' his voice hardened '—I have never lied to you, so don't insult me by saying I have.' He lifted his wine glass and reflected moonlight shimmered and danced as he idly swirled the contents. 'But that's what women do, isn't it? When they're cornered they fling out patently absurd counter-accusations.'

'You must have known a few really weird women,' Lisa replied quietly. If she allowed her voice to rise by the merest fraction she would go out of control, start to rant and rave. 'So you can take back that sexist remark and explain why you told me you were a humble waiter when all the time you were sickeningly wealthy.'

She picked up her own glass. Her hand was shaking. She put it down again before she disgraced herself and spilled the lot. Diego, leaning well back in his chair, remarked, 'You decided I was a humble waiter. I told you, quite truthfully, that I spent almost all of my evenings working in one of the hotel restaurants. You see, my tarnished angel, how I remember every word we ever said to each other? The hotel we were to meet in on that last night was the latest in the family chain. My father, being a sensible man, insisted that I had hands-on experience of each branch of the varied business enterprises. I was acting night manager at that time.'

Lisa's eyes filled with emotional tears. She couldn't help it. Her crazy heart seemed to turn to mush. He'd obviously meant to be scathing and he didn't realise what he'd just unwittingly given away—that he, too, had remembered every word they'd ever said to each other. That wouldn't happen, would it, if he'd thought of her as just a casual fling, something to amuse him and boost his inflated male ego?

She must have meant something to him… 'Why didn't you tell me who you were?' she asked shakily. 'I told you all about myself. What I mean is, I answered every question you ever asked. Why did you let me go on thinking you were scraping a living waiting on tables?' She had believed a lie and he had let her. He must have been laughing at her misconception, thinking she was a real fool. That really hurt. She had been open and frank with him and he… 'Why were you so sly?'

'Why do you think?' Diego countered grittily. 'And I'd prefer the word sensible to sly.' He put his emptied glass on the table top and Lisa blinked the recent moisture from her eyes and narrowed them at him through tangled damp lashes.

A single glass with dinner was all she'd ever seen him take but this evening he was drinking steadily. To drown his guilty conscience over his foray into the world of blackmail? Or was he seeking Dutch courage before he meted out the punishment he'd mentioned earlier? So far he'd shown no sign of wanting to have his wicked way with her!

Barely breathing at the thought of that, Lisa found it difficult to concentrate on anything else and had to force herself to tune in to him when he told her edgily, 'Since I turned seventeen I've been hunted down by females with their eyes on the main chance.' A brief silence, loaded with cynicism, then more softly, almost as if he were talking to himself, 'I rather liked the idea that you thought I was just an ordinary guy.'

Was that a hint of a smile in his voice? Lisa couldn't be sure, but hoped it was. And, prince or pauper, no one could ever call him ordinary.

And then, of course, he spoiled it all by drawling, 'You were very young. Both in years and experience. I would imagine it takes a little time for a girl to learn how to be more discriminating—financially speaking, that is—with her sexual favours.'

Still mooning over his liking her because she'd thought he hadn't got two pennies to rub together, it took Lisa several seconds to work out the implication of what he'd just casually tossed at her.

He was calling her a gold-digger!

He obviously hadn't believed a word of what she'd said about her reasons for finally agreeing to his callous proposition. He thought she'd jumped at it for what she hoped she could get out of him. Lazing around in the sun, waited on hand and foot, fabulous food, beautiful new clothes. Borrowed jewels!

She would rip the dress from her back if she could bring herself to stand in front of him in nothing but her underwear! As it was his hateful diamonds could go, she told herself in a fury of hating him for thinking she was the lowest of the low, for making her carry on loving him when he really and truly and thoroughly despised her!

Her face flaming with hectic colour, she jumped to her feet and dragged the fabulous bracelet off her wrist. The earrings followed, tossed carelessly down on the table. She would have thrown the whole lot over the edge of the terrace, to get lost in the sweetly flowering shrubs, if she hadn't known he'd stand over her with a stick while she grovelled on her hands and knees until she'd found them—even if it took ten years!

The choker was a different matter. Frustrated, angry tears spiked her lashes and coursed unheeded down her cheeks as she struggled with the awkward clasp, her soft mouth compressing into a hard straight line as if that would somehow ease the problem.

'Allow me.' Diego shifted lazily to his feet and came to stand behind her. Lisa stiffened as his deft fingers removed the choker. Every last one of her senses were unbearably sharpened when he was this close. She was achingly aware of the warmth of his body, of every breath she took, of every quickened heartbeat. A faint trembling invaded her body and she choked back a sob as, his task finished, the necklace tossed on the table, his hands cupped her shoulders as he turned her to face him, the look of male superiority swiftly turning to a slashing frown.

'I didn't mean to make you cry.'

Lisa saw his broad chest expand as he sucked in a

hollow breath. She bit down hard on her quivering bottom lip as he stroked the tears away with his fingers. Gentle fingers. Too gentle. She could feel a fresh deluge of shaming tears building up behind her eyes.

She was angry with him, furious, for bunching her in with a whole load of greedy gold-diggers, wasn't she? So why did she want to bury her head in that broad chest and sob her heart out?

'Please don't,' Diego muttered thickly as he ran a finger over her tightly compressed lips. A driven groan was wrenched from him as her mouth instinctively softened in unstoppable response, parting on a breathless loss of sanity as her glimmering eyes lifted to meld with the melting darkness of his and absorbed the messages he was sending out.

'Kiss me!'

Had that husky entreaty come from her or from him? Lisa didn't know or care as his dark head lowered, his long sensual mouth covering hers with a sweetness that made her dizzy, made her knees buckle beneath her with the wonder of it. Clinging to him, she ran her hands over the wide span of his shoulders as she pressed herself into the lithe length of him.

This was what she'd been wanting, aching for. The release from the tension of these last days came swiftly, with a cocooning sense of safety, of coming home to where she belonged after long sterile years of exile.

And then he deepened the kiss, his body taut and demanding, drugging her with an erotic expertise that harmonised with the sultry warmth of the night. Beneath her questing hands she felt his body shake and, even as his lips still ravaged the willing moistness of her mouth, his long hands swept the narrow straps of her dress off her shoulders then slid with shaky, barely contained impatience, to cup her naked breasts.

Desire, naked and unashamed, swept through her on a hot, wild tide. 'Kiss me!'

This time she knew the honeyed command had come from her, knew the intoxication of pure incandescent joy as his dark head bent to take one straining nipple between his lips and then the other. Her back arched in ecstasy, her head falling back on her neck, her fingers digging into his skull, through the thick dark softness of his hair as she held him to her.

With hot, muttered words in his own language, Diego found the delicate zipper at the back of her dress, heard the slither of silky chiffon as it pooled at her feet. With his hands on either side of her tiny waist he raised his head and held her minutely away from him, drinking in the loveliness of her.

Tiny white briefs hid her sex. Her skin gleamed like mother-of-pearl in the moonlight. Her eyes, darkened by the desire that thrummed between them, glowed for him.

Only for him…

He had to believe that…

With a smothered groan he lifted her slender pale arms from around his neck, scooped her up, holding her tightly against his racing heartbeat and carried her to his bed, where she belonged.

CHAPTER EIGHT

PALE, pure moonlight bathed Lisa's beautiful body in silvered washes as he lowered her on to his bed, the dark cover accentuating the ivory loveliness of her limbs and the silver gold of her hair, those long silky tendrils spread around her.

His heart racing, Diego straightened, his fingers moving to his shirt buttons. His hands were shaking. His body was aching for her. Just her. Only ever her. His pale, glorious angel.

He'd waited so long. Too damned long!

A soft breeze from one of the many open windows set deep in the ancient stone walls feathered over his skin as he dropped his shirt to the floor, his eyes never leaving the deep pools of hers.

Moonlight made a mystery of her. He snatched in a breath. His lungs tightened. He was about to solve that mystery.

She was his!

A tiny gasp alerted him to the fact that her eyes had broken his hypnotic hold on her and were drinking in his partial nakedness, sweeping achingly slowly across the breadth of his shoulders, down to the tightness of flat stomach muscles. A nerve jumped at the side of his hard jawline as she raised her pale slender arms to him, her lips parting on another intake of breath.

Without having to think about it, he took her outstretched hands in his and brushed his lips over the backs of her fingers, turning them over to place lingering kisses in her tender palms, just as he had always done when he'd greeted her way back in that time so long ago when love had been young and infinitely precious, the most precious thing in the world for him.

'Diego—'

Just his name, emerging from her lips on a rawly breathy sigh that could have been the desperate plea he'd been waiting for. His heart seemed to swell to twice its normal size within his chest cavity, making him breathless as his impatient, unsteady hands dropped to the waistband of his trousers and dealt summarily with the zip.

And *Madre di Dio!* Did she know what her eyes were saying to him as they rose, limpid dark pools full of yearning neediness, to lock again with his?

Leaning over her, he touched her soft lips with the tips of his fingers and she parted them with immediate, telling response, her long lashes drifting closed over those beautiful sultry eyes.

He lowered his tight, throbbing body on to the bed beside her, hot masculine pleasure flowing through him in a wild unstoppable tide as she turned to him, those delicate naked limbs reaching for him, holding him, her arms around his body, her legs entwined with his, her gloriously sexy mouth raised to his.

He wanted to lose himself in that mouth, in that exquisite body. The need was raw and primitive, but 'Slowly, my angel,' he murmured thickly, needing to savour this moment, the forerunner of the climax that had haunted his mind for far too long, savour this timeless moment before the blessed release from private nightmares of anger and frustration.

Even so, he could no more stop his hands from sweeping down the length of her body, sweeping away the tiny briefs, the final barrier between them.

He heard her soft intake of breath, felt her body shake with fine tremors as the instinctive, urgent arching of her hips met his full arousal and he knew the sting of desire was building in her, unfettered, hot and greedy, meeting his own.

His hand on the seductive curve of her hips pressed her closer and lightning forked through his loins as she moved against him, her sweet mouth trailing feverish kisses along the length of his throat.

Diego dragged in a harsh breath. This was what he'd wanted, wasn't it? Lisa's wantonly willing body in his bed, pleasuring him, washing away the years of anger and bitterness.

And yet— He wanted more. Far more than the primeval act of mating. He had no idea where the sudden need had sprung from but the power of it was an insistent beat in his brain.

Feeling her skin against his skin, the heated urgency that was melding them together, two bodies as one, had wrought a change in him, a shift in his underlying emotions. This thing—the path to revenge he'd put in train—was debasing both of them.

Knowing he could be an all-time loser, committing himself to frustrated needs, no earthly chance of redemption, Diego levered himself up on one elbow, his eyes narrowed solemnly on her lovely face.

His voice flat with the knowledge of what he was about to do, the outcome uncertain, he told her, 'The game's over, Lisa. You've kept your side of the unworthy bargain I forced on you—coming willingly to my bed—and I'll keep mine.' He shifted his weight slightly, putting an unwanted space between them and hating it, craving the ultimate closeness which now might never come. 'The magazine's safe. Your father won't have occasion to lower his new found good opinion of you.' He dragged in a harsh breath, his stomach hollow. 'And you're free to go back to your own room right now, if that's what you want, and back to London as soon as we can arrange a flight. Just say the word.'

Shock froze Lisa's body, wiped out her vocal cords. He didn't want her! She was offering and he was saying no thanks! His sole and despicable intention had been to humiliate her.

Struggling helplessly to work out what was happening here, she scoured his shadowed face with desperate eyes but found no answer, merely enigma. His moods could change faster than a teenager's. Marbella this morning. And now this.

Now that he'd proved to himself that he could bring her to the point of writhing about on his bed, naked and frantic for his love-making, he was throwing her out like the worthless object he had decided she was!

'You are one vile human being! Do you know that?' burst from her on a wild tide of really loathing him. Limbs flailing, humiliation exploding inside her, Lisa tried to struggle off the bed, get as far away from the monster as she possibly could.

'Tranquilo.' Two gently determined hands curved round her shoulders, pressing her back against the pillows. A smile mellowed his voice. 'Allow the vile human being to finish.'

At her seething snort of outrage and ineffectual struggles the smile vanished, leaving his voice ragged. 'I want you to stay. Believe me, I want it more than anything else. But only if you want it too. Without threats hanging over your head, Lisa. You don't owe me anything and if you stay with me it must be of your own free will. Otherwise, when we make love it will be meaningless. Do you understand what I'm saying?'

Poleaxed into speechlessness, Lisa lifted her hands to cup his beloved face. Her heart was suddenly so full she was sure it was about to burst. He wanted her to stay with him; he'd said so with a sincerity that made her heart ache. He wanted to make love with her, not just have sex. And he wanted it to mean something!

He did care about her. It was obvious, wasn't it? Her breath exhaled on an emotional sob. She wriggled forward, reclaiming the small unendurable space he'd put between them. Maybe he was remembering the wonderful magical times they'd shared all those years ago, was regretting having played around, one girl for the daylight hours, one for the evening. Maybe...

Expelling a driven moan, Lisa dragged his head down to hers and kissed him with a wild hunger that drew an answering blisteringly passionate response. Only when the need for breath became imperative was she able to tell him what was in her heart, her voice no more than a whisper as she confessed, 'I want to stay. I want you, Diego, I want everything back the way it was.'

'That can't happen, my angel,' Diego denied wryly, one hand gently caressing her fine-boned shoulder. 'The past can't be reclaimed, no matter how much we wish it could be. We are both older and hopefully wiser. All we can do,' he said thickly, 'is concentrate on the present.' His hand slipped lower, resting possessively on the throbbing peak of one breast then sliding to the other, the hot pleasure almost more than she could stand as her whole body was invaded by a desire so intense it shocked the breath out of her body.

'You are so beautiful. I ache for you!' His voice was ragged with emotion, more heavily accented than she had ever heard it. 'I have dreamed of this,' he confessed rawly, the touch of his hands as he explored her willing body slow and sensual, blowing her mind, making her writhe against him, her breath coming in frantic gasps until he held both her hands above her head and murmured softly, 'Patience, my angel. I am a possessive man and I will give pleasure such as you have never known.'

His black eyes smouldered with male intent. 'After tonight there will be no room in your mind for any other man.'

There had never been any other man, Lisa thought dizzily and wondered whether she should tell him, then gave up on all brain functions as his lips erotically travelled the path of his exploring hands.

She'd been a virgin; he was sure of that. She might have been a flirt and a tease, but she hadn't been promiscuous. She hadn't even slept with Clayton; he'd stake his life on it.

Looking down at her fragile, fine-boned body as at last she slept, Diego's heart swelled with an emotion he couldn't name. The triumph of male possession? A release from the devils of the past?

Love?

Love. His mouth compressed wryly. He'd loved her once, adored her, put his angel on a golden pedestal. And look where that had got him! His days of romanticising fallible womanhood were long gone.

Yet she was ineffably special; he was too honest to deny that.

Tenderly, careful not to wake her, he drew the silken cover over her body, as graceful in sleep as she always was awake, and eased himself off the bed. Fingers of dawn light were creeping into the room. Each climax had been more stunning than the last. He had never known anything like it but, in spite of all that sensual overload, he was bursting with vitality.

A long walk was called for. Something to tax his body and leave his mind free to work out his feelings, let him see the future—if there could be any future for the two of them, he amended—more clearly.

Lisa woke to floods of sunlight. She could hear the doves calling in the courtyard below, a soft sweet sound that matched her mood perfectly. Releasing herself from the tangle of the silky cover she wriggled over and stared at the empty space beside her.

Diego was already up and about. It didn't matter that he'd left her to sleep alone. She vented a dreamy sigh. He could change his mood more often than he changed his socks and that didn't matter either.

She knew what she knew.

What he felt for her went far deeper than simple male lust; she knew it did. Hadn't he offered to let her go before things went any further, hadn't he admitted he wanted her to stay, but only if she wanted it too? And throughout the long, ecstatic night he'd made love with such passionate tenderness, as if she were the most precious thing in the world!

It couldn't possibly get any better or any more revealing of his true feelings than that, could it?

Slipping out of bed, she hugged her arms around her body. She was actually squirming with happiness inside. She felt intoxicated by it. Despite what he'd said, they could recapture the past. And if he still went on denying it then she'd have to make sure to change his mind!

The embarrassing problem of getting back to her own rooms, naked, without being met by Rosa or Manuel, was solved when Diego walked into the room moments later. He was carrying something over his arm; she didn't register what because she only had eyes for him, for his heart-wrenching gorgeousness.

Those dark eyes were intimately warm, his slow smile infectious, and the way the fine cotton of his sleeveless shirt clung to the wide span of his shoulders, those long legs clothed in narrow-fitting sand-coloured jeans, made her legs go hollow, her tummy tighten with intense physical need.

Feeling the rosy peaks of her breasts swell and tingle, her pale skin bloomed with warm colour as his eyes made a languid tour of every naked inch on display.

Her eyelids drooped, she could hardly keep them open and her breath was coming in ragged little gasps. She loved him so, wanted him until she went weak and boneless from the tips of her toes to the top of her tousled head.

Diego walked towards her and then past without so much as touching her. Lisa's face fell a mile but her dismay was swiftly forgotten when he laid garments she vaguely recognised from the stuff he'd splurged out on yesterday down on the bed and turned to her, grinning wickedly over his shoulder.

'I've been retrieving last night's careless scatterings.' He straightened up, his feet planted apart, his soft, slightly breeze-ruffled black hair gleaming in the shafts of sunlight, his eyes smiling for her. 'We left your dress and a fortune in diamonds in the courtyard, remember?' A slanting brow quirked. 'Now, I don't mind the staff putting two and two together but I thought you might.' His mobile mouth curved. 'The diamonds are back in the safe and your dress is back in your room.'

And after that he'd tramped the hillside, getting his mind straight and not liking himself. He could only describe his behaviour as appalling. He'd verged on an unprecedented and shameful temper tantrum after she'd admitted that holding on to her father's approval was the only reason she'd agreed to his unholy proposition. So, not recognising what was actually happening to him when it smacked him squarely in the face, he'd set out to punish her.

He'd been falling in love with her all over again and had been too stiff-necked and blinkered to admit it to himself. He didn't care how badly she'd behaved in the past. *Madre di Dios!* She'd been little more than a child at the time!

'And this—' a lean tanned hand indicated the clothing he'd put down on the bed, drawing a steadying breath to get himself back on track '—is for you to dress in after you've showered.' He glanced at her enquiringly. 'So, breakfast in half an hour?'

At her mute nod he dipped his head understandingly and came to her, where her feet felt rooted to the polished boards, his hands thrust firmly in his trouser pockets. 'I know.' His voice lowered with husky understanding. 'But if I touch you we'll never leave that bed. And I've got plans for today. There's a cove I know of, not more than a hour's drive away. No one ever goes there. It will be just the two of us.'

He wanted to take her in his arms, feel that beautiful body trembling with need against his own, kiss her until they both forgot what planet they were on, wanted it so much that he didn't know how he managed to get himself out of that room.

But how could he talk rationally to her when they were in the throes of making love—which was what would happen if he stayed in the intimacy of the bedroom with her—naked and utterly desirable as she was?

Couldn't be done.

On the secret silvery beach, just the two of them and all the time in the world, he could open his heart to her. They could disregard all that had happened in the past and plan for the future. A long and happy future together. If she'd have him, if she could fall in love with him all over again.

And if she was having any trouble in that direction he'd make it happen for her just as it had for him, he decided with a surge of fierce Spanish possessiveness before he turned his mind to more practical matters and stalked off to find Rosa to order a lavish picnic hamper.

A tender smile on her face, Lisa couldn't move for quite some time. They were to spend the day together. Not like yesterday when he'd stalked around with a face like thunder, spending money on her as if it were an unpleasant but necessary duty. Not like the days that had gone before when they'd met only briefly at mealtimes, either. But together, really together, and loving too. Well, she was almost certain about that.

Almost.

With a guilty squawk, realising time was flying, she showered in his bathroom and scurried back to the bedroom to get into the clothes he'd so thoughtfully brought in here for her.

Gossamer fine underwear, just panties, no bra. Her face bloomed with frankly delicious lustful pleasure because the top he'd provided was definitely provocative—a fine cotton, much the same colour as her eyes, sleeveless, cut to reveal her shoulders with a sexy V neck and tiny buttons down the front. She could just imagine him undoing them, slowly, one by one.

Before those mind pictures could get the better of her she stepped into a floaty cream-coloured skirt and thrust the hem of the top under the narrow waistband, then used Diego's comb to restore her hair to its normal sleek, beyond-shoulder-length waterfall.

She was nervous as a kitten faced with a bristling Alsatian, she admitted as she stepped into the strappy sandals that completed the outfit, frightened of what the future might bring.

What if Diego saw the future as the few weeks, or mere days even, before he had to get back to his busy working life? Nothing more than a stolen interlude of fabulous sex with a very willing woman? And then: goodbye, it's been nice getting reacquainted, see you some time. Maybe.

She took a deep breath to calm herself down, told herself to stop being paranoid—she really meant something to him, didn't she?

Of course she did!

To stop herself from dwelling senselessly on the worst case scenario, she decided to spend a few minutes before joining him for breakfast taking stock of his room in daylight.

Unlike the room she'd been given, it was almost austere, dominated by the huge bed. Highly polished floorboards, no softening colourful rugs. A cavernous wardrobe, heavily carved with what appeared to be exotic fruits and vine leaves, and a solitary desk set against the wall between two of the tall windows.

Gravitating towards it, she noted the angled lamp, the pens in a horn beaker, suggesting that when he was here he sometimes wrote letters or jotted down memos for his staff before retiring for the night.

A photograph in a plain silver frame. A handsome middle-aged couple. His parents? Running her fingers over the frame, Lisa wondered if she'd ever get to meet them and tried to block out the memory of his scathing, 'There are women a man would be happy to introduce to his parents. Patently, you are not one of them.'

That had been before they had made love and found each other again. Things were very different now. Of course they were, she assured herself staunchly.

A smaller frame was half hidden behind the photograph of the smiling middle-aged couple. Curiously, Lisa slid it out into the light. And her heart literally stopped. Then crashed on. She would never forget that fascinatingly sensual face. The face of the woman she'd seen him with all those years ago. Feeling nauseous, she pushed it roughly back out of sight.

He wouldn't still keep her photograph near his bedside if she'd been simply a young man's fling, part of his wild oat sowing period, would he, part of a promiscuous past he would rather forget. She had to be someone really special to him. The knowledge left Lisa feeling cold and frightened. Had she got everything wrong? Was her heart to be broken all over again? And could she hope to survive it?

Had he married this vibrantly lovely creature? Was that why he kept her photograph beside that of his parents, part of a family group? Was he being unfaithful to his wife, treating her, Lisa, as nothing more than a piece of unfinished business?

He was used to cheating on women, wasn't he, as she knew to her cost. She should have remembered that.

Her hand flew to her trembling mouth to smother a cry of pain, the suspicions crowding in, thick and fast. And why, in the name of all that was holy, hadn't she thought to ask him, way back in London, if he was married?

She swung out of the room. It was an omission she was about to remedy. The last time, when faced by evidence of his perfidy, she had cut him brutally out of her life without telling him why.

This time it would be different.

CHAPTER NINE

CALM, at all costs she had to remain calm, Lisa repeated to herself as she trod the upper corridors of the ancient monastery, heading for the stone stairs that would take her down to the magnificent great hall.

There could be a perfectly reasonable explanation why that photograph was in Diego's bedroom, though she couldn't for the life of her think of one. But she loved him, didn't she, even if he turned out to be the selfish bastard, ruthless and cruel, that was being conjured up by all these unwanted suspicions.

Some women—herself probably first among them—were their own worst enemies! She wished she could turn love off, like a tap, but knew she couldn't.

She could have married dear, safe, trustworthy Ben and spent her life on an even keel, avoiding the shattering peaks and troughs of being madly in love with a man she couldn't trust as far as she could throw him. She desperately wanted to trust him but how could she?

Pausing on the first floor landing to allow her racing heartbeat to decelerate, she leant against the cool stone window mullion. She was going to be sensible and calm about this, not rush in hurling accusations which might be unfounded.

She was no longer a naive eighteen-year-old, fresh from a convent schoolroom, she reminded herself snippily. They were both, as Diego had stated, older and wiser. She would have to try harder to believe in him, in spite of the haunting memories of what had happened all those years ago.

She knew she'd been a darn sight longer than the half an hour Diego had given her. Nevertheless she lingered for a further few moments, her attention drawn now by a bright yellow low-slung sports car parked at a skewed angle on the gravelled approach at the front of the building.

Diego had a visitor, she deduced on a flash of irritation. What a time to pick! The planned confrontation would have to be put on hold. Which might not be such a bad thing, she reflected on consideration, beginning the final descent to the ground floor. It would give her more time to cool off and recover from the shock of finding that woman's framed photograph in Diego's bedroom.

She had no appetite for breakfast, usually taken in the courtyard, but if there was any of Rosa's excellent coffee left and still drinkable she could certainly do with a cup.

Suddenly the idea of sitting in the peaceful seclusion of the courtyard strongly appealed. Breathing in the warm scented air and listening to the melodic sound of the doves, the fountain playing into its stone basin, the rustle of the soft breeze in the leaves of the old fig tree while she waited for Diego to deal with his visitor was exactly what she needed.

Such tranquillity would surely help her to come at the situation from an adult direction?

The quickest way to her objective was through the

outer door in the library, rather than the french doors leading out of the small salon she normally used. Funny how she was finally learning her way around this maze of a building at precisely the time she might have to leave nursing a badly broken heart.

But she wouldn't think about that. Not yet anyway. It was far too negative, she informed herself tartly as she pushed open the heavy oak door. First she had to hear what Diego had to say. She might have got entirely the wrong end of the stick, which begged the question that she might have badly overreacted five years ago.

And that was the last sensible thought she had because what Diego had to say on the subject of the silver-framed photograph became academic when she saw that the subject herself was sitting at the table beneath the fig tree with floods of tears running down her beautiful face. Diego was seated opposite, leaning forward, holding her hands in both of his, talking to her, his actual words indecipherable from this distance, but the tone of his voice soothing and quite definitely placatory.

Something he said must have angered the beautiful young brunette. It happened so quickly that Lisa, rigid with the shock of what she was witnessing, could only flinch with disbelief as the other woman sprang to her feet, bristling with anger, her voice hysterically shrill. The only word she was able to pick out of the tirade of Spanish was *Perfidia!*—and wasn't perfidious one of the words she'd used herself to describe the man who'd betrayed her with this very woman five years ago?

Lisa's eyes frosted over, her stomach tying itself in knots, as she watched Diego immediately get to his feet and capture the other woman's gesticulating hands. Then, with a few murmured words—silver-tongued, lying excuses?—he pulled her into his arms and held her there, tenderly pressing her glossy dark head against his wide shoulder, rocking her gently back and forth until gradually moving her towards the door to the house.

As they disappeared inside Lisa pressed her knuckles against her mouth to stop herself from crying out. She had no idea what was going on but from where she was standing those two were very far from being casual acquaintances! The suspicion that the other woman was either his fiancée or his wife returned with a force that made her feel ill.

The only way to discover the truth was to confront them and ask. And the only way to get her leaden legs to move was to try to assure herself that this was just some misunderstanding, something that looked definitely iffy on the surface, hiding a perfectly innocent explanation. After last night it just had to be that. She wasn't going to go on torturing herself by thinking anything else. Well, was she?

Shaking inside, Lisa found herself in the great hall. The ancient stone walls seemed to freeze her right through to her bones instead of creating the usual welcome cool ambience. The silence lay like a heavy weight on her shoulders. Now she was about to begin her search for Diego and the other woman she didn't think she had the courage.

If what she couldn't help suspecting turned out to

be the truth she didn't think she could bear it. Not after last night when his love-making had made her feel like the most beautiful, desired and loved woman in the world.

Adrenalin pumping, she almost leapt out of her skin when Rosa, soft-footed in her comfy old plimsolls, appeared at her shoulder. Her pretty features had concern and condemnation written all over them. Her normal smile was notably absent. Disconcerted, Lisa told herself not to be a coward; she had to get this sorted out, of course she did. She stated, 'I'm looking for the *señor*. Do you know where he is?'

A quick frown clouded the big brown eyes. 'I am to take to them coffee and cognac and leave—*solo*—' She struggled with her rudimentary English. 'You leave also. Is bad thing when the beautiful Isabella find husband have other woman. Much explosions! The *señor* needs to be—*privado*. So you leave also?'

Leave. It was the only option, Lisa decided hollowly as Rosa disappeared to meet Diego's request for coffee and brandy. Barely able to move for the feverish pain that invaded every inch of her body, she dragged herself upstairs to the rooms she'd been given.

To allow herself to be conned by Diego once had been a dreadful mistake. To allow it to happen twice should be a capital offence!

That she hadn't known he was married was no excuse, she castigated herself wildly as she closed the door to her bedroom behind her and sagged weakly back against it, nausea a coiled knot in her stomach. She should have damned well asked.

She should have known. A man so gorgeous, sinfully sexy and rotten rich would have been snapped up years ago.

Isabella—as Rosa had named her—had obviously discovered that he had a woman holed up here with him in his self-admitted private hideout, the place the family rarely visited, where his sins, for sins they were, could be hidden.

But someone must have blown the whistle—Rosa, through a sense of family loyalty?—and the wronged wife had appeared to confront him. Demanding explanations was out of the question; she saw that now, she thought on a wave of draining exhaustion. His poor wife had enough to contend with without coming face to face with Diego's latest bit on the side.

Feeling dreadful for her part in this sordid shambles, Lisa walked unsteadily to the hanging cupboard to drag her clothes out. Just the things she'd brought with her—she never wanted to set eyes on the expensive gear he'd bought her again.

In a minute she'd change out of the pretty skirt and sexy top she was wearing. But first she had to make sure she had everything she needed. Her head was in a dreadful daze, her brain consumed by her awful discovery. If she didn't take herself firmly in hand she could well land up at the airport without the essentials, hysterical and not knowing what the hell she thought she was doing!

Tipping the contents of her handbag out on to the bed beside her suitcase and the untidy heap of clothing she'd tossed there, she sifted through what the average male would classify as junk—combs, lipstick, tissues, sundry keys, a battered appointments diary, a clutch of old letters and postcards from friends—and located her passport and her wallet. She would use her credit card to take care of the flight home but, unfortunately, she would need to beg a lift to the airport.

Would Manuel be willing to drive her? There shouldn't be too much difficulty about that, she decided sickly. Hadn't Rosa insisted she leave? The Spanish woman might be disgusted by her but she would make sure her husband facilitated that sensible outcome, if only to see the back of her.

Her fingers shaky, she carefully slotted her passport and wallet into the zipped compartment where she would know where they were, and was beginning to shovel everything else back any old how when Diego walked in.

His beautiful face was grim. His wife had obviously been giving him a hard time. Serve him right! Lisa thought, trying to ignore the stab of pain that pierced her already mangled heart. She hadn't wanted to set eyes on him again but now that she had she wasn't going to let him see how devastatingly upset she was.

'What the hell are you doing?'

'What does it look like?' Lisa muttered fiercely, wanting to strangle him. 'And there's no need to snap. It's your fault if your wife's been reading the riot act, so don't take it out on me!' She grabbed the packet of tissues and something rolled off the bed. 'Rosa, in her wisdom, told me to leave so that's what I'm doing. Eminently sensible under the circumstances, wouldn't you say?'

Straightening abruptly after automatically stooping to retrieve the object that had dropped from the bed, Diego drew a sharp breath in through his teeth. Black brows meeting, he demanded, 'Run that by me again. Why the hell should Rosa tell you to leave? By what right? And what wife? I don't have a wife!'

He sent her a dark, exasperated glance and Lisa sank down on the bed and vented a huge sigh that seemed to come up from the soles of her feet.

So that was the way he was going to play it. Lying creep! With the patron saint of liars and deceivers on his side—or patron devil, more likely—he must have persuaded the hysterical Isabella to return to whence she had come, in double quick time. Made her believe there was no other woman holed up here with him, that he was here alone to commune with nature, or some such other unlikely story.

But she wasn't that gullible. No way! 'Right,' she said through gritted teeth and shot to her feet. 'Wait here,' she growled and stalked out of the room, red flags of furious disgust flying on her cheeks as she headed for his rooms, hearing his firm footsteps following as he disregarded her instruction and came after her.

She'd wanted a few minutes on her own, away from the man she was tempted to do serious damage to. But at least this way she'd have to stay a few minutes less in this place.

Swooping into his bedroom, she homed in on the framed photograph and whipped round to face him.

He towered over her, bemusement coupled with the irritation of a man reaching the end of his tether writ large on his too-handsome features.

'This—' Lisa stabbed a forefinger at the lovely smiling face 'is the woman I saw you with in Marbella on that last evening. You were all over each other. Even Sophie said you were a real steamy couple!'

He was looming over her, his expression that of a man who had been hit over the head with a rock, but that didn't fool her, not for a single instant. 'And I found this—' again a stab at the picture of the wronged Isabella '—this morning after you'd spent the night making love to me!'

When this hatefully necessary confrontation was over, she'd probably be stupid enough to cry herself to sleep every night for a year but right at this moment anger was fuelling her blistering attack.

'I came looking for you to ask for an explanation of your obvious on-going relationship with her and there she was, having hysterics, and you were—were—' Words almost failed her in her furious need to lash out at him, but she ploughed on raggedly, 'Cuddling her and stroking her…' Her voice rose to an anguished wail. 'And Rosa told me that Isabella had exploded because she had found out you had another woman. And then Rosa told me to leave.'

Struggling to make sense of the disjointed statements that were issuing from that lushly desirable mouth was like wading through a thick fog and then emerging into bright sunlight. Diego's mouth curved with immense inner satisfaction. She was behaving like a jealous virago. *Bravo!* It had to mean she cared for him!

With one hand he reached out to take Isabella's portrait from her and became aware of something digging into the palm of the other. He opened his fist on the glitter of the hoop of tiny diamonds he'd seen her wearing on the night of her engagement party.

He dragged in a breath. It didn't mean a thing. He held it out to her. Lisa, her face going bright scarlet, snatched it and felt awful. Ben had told her to keep it as a memento of their affection and what had she done? Carelessly dropped it into the messy and cavernous depths of her handbag!

Knowing Ben it wouldn't be worth much materially, but it was worth a great deal as a token of friendship and abiding affection that had been in place for most of their lives.

Cursing herself for not taking proper care of it, she slipped it on her finger for safe-keeping and Diego, watching from suddenly narrowed eyes, told himself that her wearing another man's ring didn't mean anything, either. She was almost incandescent with rage and fierily beautiful with it and now that everything had slotted into place he couldn't blame her.

As she made to stalk past him, out of the room and, presumably, given her assumptions, out of his life, Diego clamped both hands on her slight, stiffly held shoulders and swung her round to face him.

Inky-blue eyes dealt him a slaying glance and Diego grinned. Under the circumstances it probably wasn't the wisest thing to do but he couldn't help it.

She was already bristling like a wild kitten and at any moment she would use her claws!

As a small hand rose to slap the grin off his face he captured it, slid an arm around her tiny waist and deftly deposited her on the bed, quickly joining her.

'Will you stop mauling me?' Her full lower lip jutted petulantly and the temper had gone out of her voice, replaced by grumpiness. Her breathing was short and rapid, Diego noted on a tidal wave of tenderness. And something else, he decided, as desire steamed in his blood. Was she, too, remembering what had happened for them last night in this bed? She looked fantastic. His fingers itched to undo those tiny buttons down the front of the sexy top she was wearing, to slide beneath that gauzy skirt, to claim her as his own for all time because he point-blank refused to spend the rest of his life without her…

'Mauling you isn't what I had in mind,' he affirmed thickly and felt her shudder. He stopped there, hauling himself back to the present situation.

Briskly clearing his throat, he got back on track. 'From your verbal assaults I think I've worked out what's sent you up like a volcano.' His eyes, as they rested on her defensively prickly profile, went soft with compassion. He ached to take her in his arms and make her believe he loved her, had never stopped, but he had to sort out this mess first.

'Isabella—the girl you obviously saw me with in Marbella, the girl in the photograph—is my sister. That last night, when I'd asked to meet your friends, I'd planned to explain who I was and introduce you to the only member of my family who was in Spain at that time—my parents being on an extended visit to relatives in South America.'

Disconcerted by that statement, Lisa sneaked a sideways glance. He looked really sincere. But apparent sincerity was the stock-in-trade of the con artist, wasn't it?

Huffing out a sharp breath, she returned her gaze to the uncontentious consideration of her feet. She wanted to believe him and sitting beside him on this bed wasn't the best idea in the world.

'Isabella and I met up in Marbella. She insisted on going with me when I chose the ring I intended to give you. And if you saw us and decided she was all over me, well, I guess you could have got that impression. Lisa—' he cupped her chin and turned her to face him '—my sister has been a drama queen since the day of her birth, completely over the top! She was so excited that her adored brother had gone and fallen in love, was about to get engaged, and she was determined to celebrate every inch of the way.'

He felt his bones melt as her soft lips quivered, the deep blue pools of her eyes misting over. His voice was unsteady as he mentally begged her to believe in him implicitly. 'And that same headstrong nature had her setting out in the early hours of this morning to find me, vowing she'd left Cesar, her big-shot lawyer husband, because he was having an affair with his newly appointed personal assistant.

'Utter nonsense, of course.' The ball of his thumb gently stroked away a glistening tear drop. 'I calmed her down and phoned Cesar, who was worried witless. Apparently, a so-called friend of Isabella's had told her that Cesar had been seen in one of Seville's grandest restaurants with his dazzlingly lovely new assistant when he'd told her he was working late. Well, that was exactly what he was doing, having a working dinner with an important client. His assistant was there to take notes. Nothing else. Cesar adores Isabella. The idea of cheating on her would never cross his mind.'

'That's what I did all those years ago, didn't I? Overreact. I spoiled what we had. I decided you were a penniless waiter, the sort who preys on well-heeled females for what you could get out of them,' Lisa confessed mournfully after a long beat of silence, feeling really guilty for the bad names she'd called him inside her head and sick at heart at the thought of what she'd done.

She sniffed miserably. Five years ago this fantastic man had loved her, had chosen a ring to make their engagement official and she'd ruined everything, thought the very worst of him, not giving him the opportunity to say a word, just opening her big mouth and sending him away.

'Don't cry.' Diego got to his feet to reach for a tissue from the box on the night table. Wordlessly, he handed it to her and stood over her, watching as she dabbed her eyes then pulled the soggy tissue into tiny little pieces. She was the picture of misery. His heart kicked with compassion. He knew exactly what she was feeling. He, too, savagely regretted the misunderstandings of five years ago, the barren wasted years.

But the moment passed. Brooding over what

couldn't be changed was a fool's game. Only the future mattered. As soon as Isabella was safely on her way back to Seville he would have all the time in the world to convince this adored, delicately lovely creature that he loved her more than life itself and ask her to be his wife—go down on his knees and beg if necessary! But until then… 'Can you remember how Rosa asked you to leave?' he enquired briskly of the silky crown of her drooping head. It was the one thing that was still puzzling him. His staff weren't in the habit of telling his guests what to do.

Lisa's thoughts were still on the way her awful behaviour had driven this fantastic man away. Not only that of five years ago but this morning too. He was proud and honourable; he wouldn't relish the idea of being thought of, firstly, as some sort of gigolo and then as a cheating, sneaky husband. Last night she had really believed he cared for her, that they could put the past behind them and start over. Right now he would be despising her, or thinking she was completely insane. He would want to see the back of her as soon as possible.

'You can't remember?' Diego asked with a decisive bite.

Lisa shivered. He was out of patience with her and she couldn't blame him. 'Oh, that.' She recalled his question and mumbled, almost word for word, what Rosa had said, then gasped with surprise as his strong hands fastened around her waist and pulled her upright.

'Rosa has some difficulties with the English language. I'd asked her to bring coffee and brandy and then make sure that Isabella and I were left alone, and to pass that message on to you with my apologies. I needed time to quieten her down and contact Cesar. She didn't mean you were to leave the house.'

Lisa nodded, helplessly acknowledging that she was pretty damn good at getting her wires crossed. And driving a huge wedge between herself and the man she loved to distraction.

'Right,' Diego said flatly, for the first time in his life wishing his sister hadn't followed the habit of a lifetime and come running to him whenever something happened to upset her. He wanted her out of the way, well out of it, to begin his campaign to get Lisa to agree to marry him. 'Let's get you looking less like a wet weekend, then go and keep Isabella company.'

Impersonal hands smoothed her hair off her face while he was telling her, 'Cesar's already on his way to collect her. He's bringing one of his junior clerks to drive her car back. He refuses to let her get behind the wheel when she's in a state, which,' he admitted drily, 'she mostly is. Either deliriously happy, high as a kite, or down in the rock-bottom dumps.'

His mouth tightened as he tucked the wandering hem of her top back into the waistband of her skirt. The touch of her skin scalded him. *Dio!* He didn't know how he stopped himself from taking her in his arms and smothering her with burning kisses. He would make up for it later, when they were alone.

Lisa noted the compression of his beautiful mouth and the chilling fact that there was no reaction to the small intimacy. She bit down hard on her lower lip to stop herself from weeping. The magic they'd re-captured last night had clearly gone and was lost for ever, swept away by her not trusting him and thinking the sort of things about him that no man could be expected to ever forgive.

'In the meantime we could all use some breakfast.' He made a terse after-you gesture in the direction of the door and Lisa exited, trying not to look as down as she felt.

Watching the unconsciously sensual sway of her hips as she walked out of the room Diego smothered a groan. Part of him wanted to haul her back and open his heart to her, confess that he couldn't rest until she'd given her word that she would spend the rest of her life with him.

But the more sensible part insisted that he would need more than a few rushed minutes to convince her that despite his sordid and shamefully dishonourable attempts at revenge he did truly love her.

A decision he would later deeply regret.

CHAPTER TEN

THEY found Isabella sprawled out on a padded sun-lounger on the terrace. As Diego's shadow fell across her she half opened her dark sleepy eyes and murmured plaintively, *'Tengo mucha hambre!'*

'Speak English, *cara*. We have a guest.'

There was no mistaking the affection in his tone, in stark contrast to the snippy way he'd been speaking to her, Lisa recognised wretchedly.

'We are all hungry, breakfast has been delayed for too long,' he chided gently as he took his sister's slim hands and helped her to her feet. 'Isabella, meet Lisa Pennington,' he introduced smoothly, his smile for his sister.

Feeling like a spare part, Lisa met Isabella's wide smile and returned it feebly. There was no sign now of that earlier hysterical anger, just a warm look of curiosity on that vivacious face.

'*Hola! Lo siento*—I forgot—no Spanish! You are English, yes?' She tucked her arm through Diego's, her curvaceous body in flame-coloured linen pants topped by a white silk blouse gracefully relaxed as she gave Lisa a warm assessment. 'You are the secret one, my brother, to hide your guest here away from prying eyes!'

Her sultry eyes, glinting with mischief, found Lisa's. 'So tell me, how did you do it? Diego's so off women it's painful. It's lovely to see he can be as human as the rest of us—and wicked, too! Tell me, is my big brother truly wicked?'

'Lisa's father is a recently acquired business partner. She is part of the same enterprise,' Diego cut in repressively. 'You said you were hungry.' He curtly dismissed the subject of Lisa's status. 'So why don't we eat?'

Give Isabella the merest hint of a romance in the offing and she would be merciless, as he remembered only too well. The outrageous teasing and non-stop questions when he'd invited her to Marbella to meet his intended fiancée five years ago had tried his patience to the limits. He and Lisa had to sort things out for themselves. And they needed to be alone.

'Oh, just business,' Isabella said disappointedly as Diego steered her back towards the house. 'How horribly boring.'

Lisa followed on leaden legs. Diego was cutting her out of his life, that much was painfully obvious. But what else could she have expected after the things she'd accused him of? His Spanish pride wouldn't forget such insults to his integrity.

She had woken to a day that had seemed to be so full of promise, sure that they could reclaim the joyous, loving happiness they had both thought they'd lost. Now there would be no lazing about on the beach he had spoken of, no making love, no talking, no way of discovering if he really did still care for her.

Her shoulders slumped and not even the Spanish sun burning into her back could thaw the ice that was forming around her heart. If he had started to believe that there was still something very special between them, then she'd certainly put paid to that by opening her big mouth on a spate of wild accusations. It certainly looked that way from where she was standing and she couldn't come out with it and ask, not with Isabella around.

Following the other two, Lisa took her place at the table in the small salon where Rosa had produced dishes of scrambled eggs and mushrooms, the usual crusty rolls with a choice of fillings, cured ham, crisp sweet tomatoes, cheese and anchovies.

'I am dying of hunger!' Isabella declared theatrically, opening her starched white napkin with a flourish. 'All my own fault, of course. I couldn't eat a thing after I believed my darling Cesar was betraying me with another! How could I have been so silly? He will be so cross with me. I shudder!'

She didn't seem exactly fazed by the prospect, Lisa thought tiredly as she took a roll she didn't want and began to crumble it on her plate. Diego didn't appear to have much appetite, either. He just sliced a tomato up on his plate and drank several cups of coffee.

Rousing herself to make an effort—it was entirely her own fault that Diego had washed his hands of her so she had to accept it and not wallow in self-pity and sit here like a mute lump of misery—she asked over-brightly, 'What time do you expect your husband, Isabella?' She guessed that Diego would remain politely distant with her until they were alone again, then arrange for her own departure in double quick time.

'Diego?' Isabella had polished off the eggs and was piling a roll with thin slices of ham. 'What do you think? Mid-afternoon?'

'Maybe sooner.'

Dio! The sooner the better! If he'd had his wits about him earlier he'd have told Cesar he'd drive his scatty wife back to Seville himself. At least he'd have been doing something constructive. Instead of just sitting around waiting, carefully not looking at Lisa because when he did he had a battle royal on his hands, wanting to pull her into his arms and kiss her until she agreed to be his wife. He could have insisted she came with them, so that she'd have no opportunity to leave, as she'd been on the point of doing.

Edgily, he pushed back his chair and got to his feet, his hard jawline grim. Isabella dabbed her mouth with her napkin and said, 'Are you in a bad temper? Am I being a nuisance? Do tell if I am.' She tilted her head coquettishly, her accompanying smile saying she couldn't believe she could possibly have any nuisance value to anyone. 'If you and Lisa want to have your business meeting, or whatever, then please go ahead. I won't listen if it's supposed to be secret!'

'My discussions with Lisa can wait,' he answered tersely. Taking up that suggestion, whisking Lisa away for a bogus business meeting in the library, was more than tempting. But he couldn't trust his inquisitive, easily bored sister not to barge in on them. Probably at a critical moment. So he'd just have to curb his impatience, grit his teeth and wait it out.

He said, 'I'll ask Rosa to take fresh coffee to the courtyard. I'll join you there shortly.'

Watching his smooth stride, the proud angle of his handsome head as he walked from the room, Lisa felt her eyes blur with tears. She knew what form the discussion he'd mentioned would take.

Would he accept her heartfelt apologies? Probably. With a formal, chilling courtesy. But all the grovelling apologies in the world wouldn't change a single thing. The damage had been done. His current attitude towards her, the way he deliberately refused to even look at her was proof of that.

'Pouff!' Isabella patted her slender midriff. 'I eat too much. I soon will burst! Shall we do as ordered?' She tucked her arm through Lisa's as they both rose from the table. As they strolled together to the inner courtyard Lisa knew that under any other circumstances she would have enjoyed this woman's lively company. They might have become really good friends.

Pausing by the central fountain, gently splashing into the shallow stone basin, Isabella dabbled her fingers in the cool water. 'I am always telling Diego he must have a pool put in this place. At least then there would be something to do.' She shrugged her elegant shoulders. 'But he always tells me something so modern wouldn't fit the whatever you call it—*ambiente*.'

'Atmosphere?' Lisa supplied gently. 'I think he's right. There's something so timeless about this ancient place. It would be a pity to spoil it. '

'Then I am outnumbered! Diego must be right when he calls me a barbarian!' Her wide white grin was stunningly unrepentant. 'But of course he has the swimming pool at his so modern home near Jerez. I am surprised he didn't invite you there for your business meeting. Or book you into a hotel, one belonging to our family, naturally, as is usual with his business associates.'

The dark eyes were dancing with sardonic little lights but Lisa managed a throwaway shrug as if she didn't understand what Isabella was getting at. But of course she did. She obviously had her doubts about her brother's assertion that Lisa's presence here at his isolated and private hideaway had something to do with her father's business.

The water danced with flashing lights. The sun beat down on her head. The paving stones seemed to tilt beneath her feet. The scent of the flowers that rambled over the old stone walls and billowed from the dozens of planters was suddenly overpowering. Lisa raised an unsteady hand to her temple. She was feeling strangely dizzy. She should have forced herself to eat something...

'Oh—you are engaged to be married?'

Did Isabella sound disappointed? Not possible, surely? She had to be imagining it. Lisa's aching brow pleated as the other girl took her hand and examined Ben's ring. She had forgotten she was wearing it. It was nothing like as grand as the huge emerald Isabella sported next to her wide gold wedding band.

'So when is the big day? Are you soon to be married? To an Englishman back home? Or to someone else, someone I might know?' the Spanish girl enquired archly.

'Sorry?' Lisa's eyes clouded as she attempted to

sift through the spate of questions with a brain that was suddenly assaulted by a headache of unprecedentedly vicious proportions.

'Are you to marry your Englishman soon?' Isabella persisted as Rosa appeared at the far side of the courtyard to deposit a tray of fresh coffee on the table beneath the fig tree.

'Yes,' Lisa stated as firmly as she could, given the way she was feeling—all wobbly and feeble, her head pounding. It was a silly weak lie, of course, but it should stem the spate of eager intrusive questions. Saying no would involve explanations about the broken engagement, her reasons for still wearing her ex-fiancé's ring, explanations that she didn't feel up to making right now. She felt with draining misery that she would never want to talk to anyone about anything ever again.

'Move into the shade.' Diego's command was ferociously taut. The sound of it, right behind her, made Lisa jump out of her skin.

Had he heard that stupid lie? More than likely. Her heart lurched downwards at the speed of an out-of-control lift. But she could explain later, of course she could. She twisted her head, seeking his eyes, but he was already walking Isabella to the table.

If he had heard, and he must have done—she'd spoken the lie firmly and he wasn't deaf—it certainly wasn't bothering him one little bit. He was smiling and looking sveltely relaxed as he held out a chair for his sister. As far as he was concerned she could go and marry the devil himself. She had never felt so utterly wretched.

Diego's face ached from smiling and responding to Isabella's idle chit-chat. And his heart ached because of what he'd heard.

She couldn't still be planning to marry Ben Clayton. He wouldn't let it happen! He must have got hold of the wrong end of the conversation. They couldn't have made love with such passion, tenderness and beauty if she'd been in love with another man.

Lisa wasn't that kind of woman.

Unless... The unwelcome thought darkened his soul and made his blood run cold. Unless they'd cooked something up between them.

Faced with the failure of the magazine, their parents facing a mountain of debts, both of them about to lose what they probably thought of as their inheritance, not to mention their jobs, he could almost hear Clayton telling her, Do this for us, for our future. Do what he wants, lie back and think of *Lifestyle* flourishing again. And when he throws you out we'll marry anyway.

Utter nonsense!

He wouldn't let himself go down the tortuous track Lisa had followed earlier when she'd believed Isabella was his wife. In view of what Rosa had said to her he could understand why she'd jumped to that conclusion. Coupled with the misconceptions of five years ago he could understand and forgive.

But she'd been kissing Clayton as if she couldn't wait to jump into bed with him.

He wished he hadn't had to remember the torrid

scene that had left him feeling so shattered, the shock quickly turning to bitterness and anger.

In any case, she had never been to bed with Clayton. He knew that for a fact. She'd been a virgin; he'd stake his life on it.

She'd been angry enough to slay him where he stood when she'd accused him of being married. If she was in love with Clayton, if together they'd hatched up the plan to part him from a sizeable chunk of money, then the fact that he had made her his bit on the side wouldn't anger her so much, would it?

Dio! If he didn't haul her away to somewhere private within the next few minutes he'd go loco! He needed everything straightened out. He had to know if her feelings for him ran as deep as his did for her.

Brooding eyes rested on her for longer than he'd allowed himself thus far. Sideways glances, swift and quickly away again, had revealed her—unusually—adding dollops of cream and several spoonfuls of sugar into her coffee. And she'd drunk thirstily of the jug of iced water Rosa had provided. She'd been worryingly pale when she'd joined them in the shade but, thankfully, she looked marginally better now.

He loved her so much—he adored her. His heart turned over. She was listening to Isabella's rapturous descriptions of the delights of Seville, predictably focusing exclusively on the best boutiques, restaurants and night spots. The Plaza de Espana, the Giralda, the lovely gardens of the Maria Luisa Park not rating a mention. Lisa was doing her best to look interested, smiling, inserting the odd comment or question when she could get a word in but her beautiful eyes were troubled.

Time to butt in, make his excuses to Isabella and take Lisa some place where they wouldn't be disturbed. To the coast, as he'd originally planned. Isabella could kick her heels here until Cesar arrived. A just punishment for the earlier histrionics that had come within a whisker of ruining his life!

Lisa could feel Diego's eyes on her. She felt her cheeks go pink, tried to concentrate on what Isabella was chattering about, blissfully unaware of any undercurrents, and couldn't. Wondering what he was thinking, she gave a start of surprise as Rosa appeared with a portable phone extension and handed it to her.

'For me?'

Stupid question! Why else would Rosa bring the phone to her?

Her stomach lurched sickeningly. She had insisted Diego left a contact number with her father in case he wanted to get in touch with her, just for a chat, but secretly aware that he wouldn't. As far as he was concerned, if his daughter was out of sight she was out of mind.

Her hand was shaking as she took the instrument. Had something terrible happened to him? The headache that had eased while she'd been sitting in the shade came crashing back.

She spoke her name on a near whisper and heard Sophie's voice—loud, clear and riven with tension.

'Ben's been in a traffic accident. They're operating on him now. And the last thing he said before he went through to theatre was, 'Ask Lisa to come. I need to see her.' So you'd better forget what you're doing over there...' Her old friend's voice curled with contempt. 'And get back here. You owe him that much. We thought he was dying, and he still might, and I don't think it's a coincidence that a man who was always an ultra careful driver should turn into the opposite after he'd been dumped, do you?'

Too shocked to speak, Lisa's lips moved wordlessly. She could hardly take it in. Dear Ben, the lifelong friend who'd been looking out for her for years, might be dying! He mustn't!

Crisply, Sophie named the London hospital he was in then snapped, 'Say something, why don't you? Even if it's only sorry!'

Lisa snatched in a breath, anxiety making her voice thin. 'Tell him I'll be with him as soon as I can. I'll get the first available flight back. And tell him to—' her words wobbled emotionally '—hang on in there and—and wait for me.'

If he died it would be like losing a brother. And Sophie, who had been like a loving sister to her, would always lay the blame on her.

She scrambled to her feet, the phone slipping from her nerveless fingers. Trying to keep the panic out of her voice, she told the wide-eyed Isabella, 'Excuse me, I have to go.' She shot a glance in Diego's direction, noted that he'd picked up the phone and was saying something to Sophie, and fled to her room.

Once there she had to take deep breaths and really force herself to think straight, get a grip. Someone would have to drive her to the airport or arrange for a taxi. And, more importantly, she would have to say goodbye to Diego and explain what was happening.

Although, as he'd been speaking to the distraught Sophie, he would already know. There wouldn't be a problem with him. From his recent attitude towards her, he would have packed her off home as soon as he decently could in any case. This crisis merely meant that she'd be leaving a few hours earlier than he'd anticipated.

The very thought of saying goodbye to Diego made her want to throw herself on the bed and cry her eyes out. Courtesy of her nasty suspicious mind she had lost him, she knew that. Tears coursed down her pale cheeks as she began to push the things she'd thrown down on the bed earlier into the waiting suitcase.

She would have liked to have had the opportunity to apologise, to tell him she would regret everything—from her awful behaviour five years ago to the latest tantrum of suspicious abuse—for the rest of her life.

The thought that the little box she'd seen him push into his pocket in that hotel reception area had contained the ring he'd meant to give her had her hating herself. A huge sob built up inside her, venting as Diego walked into her room.

Her heart juddered to a halt and then rushed on in a panicky catch-up exercise. He looked so tense, his dark eyes glittering, his wide shoulders rigid. He was so perfect. And she'd lost him! Another sob exploded within her chest and, before she could tell him how much she regretted everything, Diego said flatly, 'I was sorry to hear the bad news. You and his family must be terribly anxious.'

The predictable words of sympathy increased the pain even more. Guilt stabbed at her heart, reminding her of how selfish she was being—crying because she'd lost whatever chance she might have had of Diego falling back into love with her when her dear friend was fighting for his life back home.

Memories of Ben's many kindnesses, the way he'd always been her ally, taking her firmly under his wing after her mother had died and her father had as good as abandoned her, came rushing back. She might have shared Sophie's amusement at his old-fashioned pedantic ways but there had always been an underlying staunch affection.

Diego, his sensational features flatly expressionless, asked, 'Do you love him?' The stark guilt of thinking only of her own utter misery regarding her fraught relationship—ex-relationship—with the man she would love for the rest of her life had the words, 'Of course I do!' tumbling in a driven wail from her tremulous lips.

His eyes glittering with pain, Diego turned. He had had to know and now his worst nightmare was staring him in the face.

How long would she have kept the pretence up? Coming willingly to his bed, even after he had told her, in a crisis of conscience, that she was free to go. How long, if the co-author of their plan to make a fool of him, take him for all they could get—the man she admitted she loved—hadn't called her back from what he must have believed was his deathbed?

Reaching the door, he turned back. The sight of her tears for the man she loved sent a cold shaft of pain through the centre of his heart. The last words he would ever say to his cheating fallen angel were, 'Manuel will drive you to the airport. Take your case down. He will be ready when you are.'

CHAPTER ELEVEN

SHE'D been fortunate with her flight but even so it was late when the taxi deposited her outside the hospital. Praying Ben had come through the operation successfully, Lisa dragged herself and her suitcase towards the main building on legs that felt too limp to hold her.

Even if he was well enough to have a visitor it was too late to see him now but she could find out how he was. Surely someone would tell her, even if she wasn't a close relative.

If Diego had been with her he would have got all the information going. He was that kind of man. He had natural authority. Her heart gave a painful twist. She had to stop thinking of him, beating herself up over what had happened; if she didn't she would go to pieces.

Nearing the double automatic doors she saw them slide open in front of the Claytons—Honor, Arthur and Sophie—who were exiting together. Lisa's heart banged frantically inside her ribcage.

After Sophie's phone call she knew they were blaming her for what had happened. She had to face them as bravely as she could. Automatically, she straightened her shoulders as they walked towards her, her heart clenching with compassion when she saw Honor's red-rimmed eyes and Sophie's drooping mouth.

'How is he?' Anxiety streaked her voice; she was dreading having to hear the worst.

'The operation was successful, thank heavens. He'll probably walk with a limp for the rest of his life but he won't lose his leg.' It was Ben's father who answered. His voice was heavy with strain and his big shoulders were slumped.

'He will be all right, though?'

'He is sleeping. We were only allowed to look in on him for a few moments,' Ben's mother put in. Honor Clayton looked a decade older than the last time Lisa had seen her at the engagement party. 'Tomorrow, all being well, we will be able to see him for a few minutes longer. It was, was—' she stumbled over the words '—good of you to come so quickly.'

Lisa shivered as a chill wind flicked her skirt against her body as she dipped her head in wordless acknowledgement of Honor's thanks, suddenly aware of the way she was dressed.

She had meant to change into practical jeans and a shirt but she hadn't had a coherent thought in her head after Diego had simply walked out on her, not giving her a chance to say she was deeply sorry for everything. In the light skirt and skimpy top she wasn't dressed for a chilly spring evening in England.

'Well, we can't stand out here getting cold.' It was Honor who rallied. 'We've persuaded Sophie to stay with us until Ben's over the worst. You must, too. You can use your old room.'

Lisa instinctively shook her head. How could she

accept their hospitality when they blamed her for being the indirect cause of Ben's accident? They were going through enough without having to endure her surely unwanted presence.

'Please come.' Sophie spoke for the first time. 'We want you to. Really we do.'

Inky-blue eyes met tearful hazel. 'Honestly?'

Sophie nodded vigorously, too choked to speak, and Arthur settled the matter, taking her suitcase and dropping a hand on her shoulder. 'Let's get to the car. There's no point hanging around here. There's nothing we can do. What we all need is a stiff drink.'

For all her school holidays after her mother's death, and that first year when she'd been working at *Lifestyle*, this room had been hers. It hadn't changed at all. The same pretty wallpaper, matching curtains and bedcover, the same white scatter rugs here and there on the pale blue fitted carpet.

She'd expected it to be quite different, for Honor to have altered the young-girl decor after she and Sophie—to Ben's irritation—had made a bid for independence and moved into the rented flat.

Somehow it didn't seem right that anything could remain so completely unchanged when her whole life had altered so drastically.

She opened her suitcase, looking for her washbag. She felt so tired, so emotionally drained, she scarcely knew what she was doing.

It had been a busy, emotional evening. While Arthur had fielded a spate of phone calls from people anxious to learn how Ben was, she and Honor had retired to the kitchen to heat soup and make toast while Sophie had located her father's single malt and given them all a more than generous tot.

The conversation, inevitably, had centred on Ben's accident. 'Apparently, he overtook a lorry on a blind bend and met a van sideways on.' Honor shuddered violently, her hand visibly shaking as she lifted the glass to her lips. 'As the police said, if he hadn't managed to swerve at the very last moment it could have been so much worse. The van driver was relatively unscathed. But Ben wasn't wearing his seat-belt. I simply can't understand it. He's always been a sensible driver.'

Inevitably, Lisa had met Sophie's eyes. She knew what her old friend thought. But the other girl compressed her lips and shook her head, tears flooding her eyes.

After the scratch meal at the kitchen table Sophie had pushed back her chair, glancing at her watch. 'James should be back by now. He's been to the Practice Manager's leaving do. He said he'd back out of it, but I told him not to. There was nothing he could do to help Ben. But I promised to phone and give him what news there is.'

Smothering a yawn, Sophie had left the kitchen and, after helping Honor load the dishwasher, Lisa had excused herself and gone to her old room.

And wished she hadn't. Downstairs, with the others, while the talk had been all of Ben and the dozens of concerned family friends who had phoned, her mind had been kept occupied by thoughts of the anxiety these good people were trying to handle.

Now, alone, her thoughts returned to her own misery. She knew it was selfish but she simply couldn't help it. What was Diego thinking of her? Had he believed the stupid lie he must have overheard? Had he misconstrued her distress on hearing of Ben's accident?

Naturally, she'd been distressed. Ben was a very dear friend of longstanding. But Diego hadn't known the full story or understood how wretchedly guilty Sophie had made her feel, piling on the sense of responsibility, increasing her need to get back to England immediately because the badly injured Ben had been asking for her. He hadn't known, or been able to understand, because he hadn't given her the opportunity to explain anything at all.

Or didn't any of that merit room in his head? Had he already decided he wanted nothing more to do with her after what she'd accused him of? Remembering the distance he'd put between them after she'd confessed to her unthinking overreaction it seemed the more likely scenario.

In any case this anguished introspection wasn't going to make anything better, was it?

'Can I come in?' Sophie, after a moment's hesitation, thrust herself into the room and two seconds later Lisa was being grabbed in a bear hug. 'I'm so sorry, Lise! What I said on the phone was hateful! Will you ever forgive me?'

'Forget it,' Lisa said with the little breath that was left in her lungs. 'I have. You were upset—'

'No, I was hateful!' Sophie denied vehemently, releasing her, standing back a pace, her eyes brimming.

'I was upset—distraught, more like it—but that didn't mean I had to lay a guilt trip on my best friend!'

Best friend!

The first warmth she'd felt since she'd woken this morning stole round her heart. Lisa gave Sophie a gentle shove that deposited her at the end of the bed and plonked herself down on the pillows, her legs tucked beneath her. Just like old times, gossiping half the night away, she thought with a clutch of gratitude at her heartstrings.

'When I thought my twin was going to die and Dad asked me to get the number from your father and phone you and tell you Ben had been asking for you, I simply let rip and lashed out. I was about to lose my brother, or so I thought, and you were swanning around in the sun with your Spanish hunk. It was unfair and wrong and I'll never be able to apologise enough.

'I was fed up with you when you broke your engagement.' Sophie gave a noisy sniff. 'I'd wanted you to be sort of cemented in our family. But Ben did explain at the time, after you'd decided to take off for Spain, that you and he had been going to settle for a dead boring marriage—my description, not his. No passion.' She was twisting the hem of her sweater between her fingers, her eyes downcast. 'Then you met up with the only real love of your life again and bingo!' She raised red-rimmed apologetic eyes. 'I'm crazy in love with James, so I do understand what happened.'

'Shut up!' Lisa said gently, swallowing a lump in

her throat. At least she had her best friend back and that was a lot to be thankful for.

Sophie asked, 'How's it going with your Spanish hunk? We thought he might have been coming with you. We got the guest room ready, just in case. Mum was determined to get you to stay with us here and not be alone in our miserable little flat.' She gave a tiny sigh. 'I expect you'll be haring back as soon as Ben's out of danger.'

Lisa firmly changed the painful subject. 'Never mind all that. Let's talk about you and James. Tell me, how's the house-hunting going? Is everything still on track for a midsummer wedding?'

No way could she discuss what had happened between her and Diego. Maybe she'd be able to confide in her friend later, when the pain of it was a little less savage. But not now.

It was two days before Ben was allowed visitors for longer than a few minutes. On the third morning he'd been moved out of ICU and into a private room and his parents and his twin visited for half an hour and reported good progress. Confined to bed with a cage over the lower half of his body, he was getting bored and cranky which, Honor said happily, meant he was well on the mend.

The atmosphere lightened dramatically and when Lisa left for the early evening session Sophie and Honor were preparing a celebratory meal of roast beef and Arthur's favourite apple pie. Her father had made daily phone calls to the Claytons to keep up to speed over Ben's progress. He'd spoken to her once, just to say he'd heard she was back and hoped Raffacani wasn't too put out by her departure. He hadn't suggested they meet. Lisa hadn't expected him to and for the first time in her life had no room in her heart for disappointment.

Lisa approached Ben's bedside with some trepidation. She couldn't imagine why she had been uppermost in his thoughts when he'd thought he might be dying. But she kept a smile on her face and it widened when she announced with genuine pleasure, 'You're looking a whole heap better than I thought you would.' She bent to kiss his cheek, laying the flowers she'd brought on his bedside locker.

'You shouldn't have bothered.' He indicated the bright bouquets in vases on every available surface. 'You only needed to bring yourself.'

'Right.' Lisa took her time locating a chair and bringing it to the bedside. *In extremis*, he had called out for her and he was going to tell her why. She dreaded hearing he had been deeply in love with her all along but had done the decent thing and stood aside when he rightly concluded she was in love with another man. Truly, shc had never wanted to hurt him.

He had never given the smallest sign that that was the case, though. She would never have agreed to marry him if she'd thought for one moment that he was madly in love with her. But some people were experts when it came to hiding their feelings.

'Well, I'm here now,' she said quietly as she sank down on the chair. 'So why did you ask to see me when you thought you might die?'

He shot her a shame-faced look and too quickly

denied thinking any such thing. 'Who said anything about dying? Other people might have been weeping and wailing and thinking the worst but I knew I'd be OK,' he said, not really convincingly. 'Got a lot to live for, haven't I?' His voice strengthened with relief as he informed her, 'I only got a smashed up leg—they've put metal pins in it—the rest of the injuries were pretty small beer, apparently, so I was luckier than I thought I was. No, the timing might have been a bit off, under the fraught circumstances, but I'd been going to ask your father for the phone number. I hadn't got around to it and it was playing on my mind.'

His hand reached for hers and gave it a friendly pat. 'I'd been worrying about you and I wanted to find out if you were OK, that Raffacani was treating you right. I had a pretty good idea of your feelings for him, but I was a bit unsure about him. I mean—a guy who would tell you, Come and live with me, or else—it made me more uneasy the more I thought about it, I guess.'

He gave her a wry smile. 'I've got too used to looking out for you. And the habit sticks. I wanted to let you know not to be afraid of coming back if things weren't working out. I would make the Dads give you a job on the staff again so you wouldn't need to be afraid of being out of work. And, knowing you, I knew you'd be feeling you wouldn't be welcome. I admit the folks were cut up when I told them the engagement was off. I explained why—though not about Raffacani's threat to cancel all his advertising—

and they came round. I wanted to let you know that we'd all welcome you back, if the need arose.'

'You're a good friend, Ben. The best,' Lisa said huskily, her eyes filling emotionally. She blinked rapidly and noticed his increasing pallor with a stab of guilt for allowing him to say so much. 'I should go; you're beginning to look tired. I've kept you talking for too long. I'll visit tomorrow if it's OK with the family.'

She got to her feet. As well as tiring him she knew that the natural progression from what he'd already said, bless him, would be to question her about her relationship with Diego.

Her non-existent relationship.

She wasn't yet up to discussing it with anyone, not even her dearest friends, without making a complete and utter fool of herself.

But Ben twisted his head on the pillow. 'Stay. I get so bored! They won't come to throw you out for at least another ten minutes.'

He looked so aggrieved she didn't have the heart to leave. But she had to keep the conversation away from her ruined relationship with Diego somehow.

So, sinking back on the chair again, she said quickly, 'Then you've got ten minutes to explain why you've started to show boy racer tendencies. Sophie and I always complained that you drove like an old granny on her way to the shops! No one can understand why you did what you did.'

Ben pulled a face, clearly embarrassed. 'It won't happen again, believe me! At the time of my accident my mind was away on another planet.'

On another planet? She said softly, 'That's not like you, Ben. You always have your feet well grounded.'

'Don't I know it!' His face turned fiercely red, alarming Lisa until he told her, 'I never thought I'd go and fall in love, but one look at her did it. It shook me rigid!'

'Ben!' Happiness for him brought the first real smile for days to her lips. 'Good for you! Who is she?'

'Sarah Davies.' He spoke the name with hushed reverence. 'You won't know her, of course. She's one of the high-flyers Raffacani brought in. She edits the gardening section—we're broadening out, not just concentrating on way out fashions very few could wear or afford and society functions of no real interest to the majority of readers.'

'And does she feel the same?' Lisa steeled herself to ask. The last thing she wanted was to see him hurt. A man who up until now had staunchly pooh-poohed the idea of romantic, passionate love could be hurt so much more than a man who had been regularly falling in and out of that state since his teens.

Ben shrugged, wincing as a minor chest injury protested. 'How would I know? Though when I finally plucked up the courage to ask her to have dinner with me she did look pleased. It was to have been the night of the accident, would you believe? My mind just wasn't on what I was doing. I was all knotted up, wondering how I should play it—no practice in that sort of thing, as you know. And there I was, knocked sideways by a big white van! I guessed I'd well and truly blown it, until this came.' He tipped his head in the direction of a get well card prominently displayed on the locker. 'Read what she's put and tell me what you think.'

'That she's holding you to that dinner date and hoping to visit you as soon as she gets the nod,' Lisa affirmed after reading the cheery message. She got up and put the card in his hands. 'I don't think you've blown it. In fact I'm sure you haven't.'

Leaning over, she put a careful kiss on his forehead. 'And, as for how to play it—don't even think about it. Just follow your heart and do what it tells you.'

Diego paced the terrace, the moon-silvered stone walls of the ancient monastery behind him offering no refuge from his tortured thoughts.

There had been no closure. Their brief time together had been meant to heal old wounds but had opened up new ones, wounds so raw and painful he could neither sleep at night nor rest by day.

He'd told himself he could put it all behind him, forget her, get on with his life. It hadn't worked. He didn't want to return to his home in Jerez, or get back to work, or stay on here.

He wanted to be with her. With Lisa. He needed her. Whatever her faults, he had to have her in his life, convince her he could make her happier than Clayton ever could.

And to accomplish that he had to do something about it. He had to go and get her, make her see they were meant to be together. It had been fated ever since he'd lifted her to her feet on that mountain track five years ago and first looked into her beautiful eyes. He'd been a lost man ever since and was damned well going to find himself again. With her. Only her.

Swinging on his heel, he stalked back into his favourite home, took the stairs two at a time and began to pack the few things he'd need. First thing tomorrow he'd be on the first available flight to London.

CHAPTER TWELVE

THE flocks of butterflies in Lisa's stomach began to beat their fluttery wings as the hired Seat climbed to the upper reaches of the twisty mountain road.

She was doing the right thing. She was! She had to hang on to that belief or she would find herself turning round in the next pull-in she came to and heading straight back to Seville.

A detailed map of the area was spread out on the passenger seat but she'd only really needed it at the start of the journey from the airport. It was as if she had an internal homing device that was drawing her back towards the man she loved.

Easing the car round a particularly tight bend she recognised the glimpse of spectacular scenery—the mountainside dropping to a deep river valley, the huddle of white-washed houses far below enclosed by the verdant greenery of vines, citrus trees and olives.

As the road widened slightly it began to descend and the butterflies cranked up their annoying activities, her neck and shoulders ached with tension and, despite the car's air-conditioning system, Lisa began to sweat. Another mile, maybe two, and she would reach the monastery. And Diego.

But she was doing the right thing!

Reaching the Claytons' Holland Park home after visiting Ben yesterday evening, the words she'd said to him had echoed with startling, inescapable clarity inside her head.

'Just follow your heart and do what it tells you.'

She had stood as still as a stone on the doorstep, listening. And her heart had told her to return to Spain, find Diego, and tell him how much she loved him. The voice was clear, insistent.

Her body had glowed—every vein, every nerve end, every muscle and sinew responding to the inescapable tug of him, as if he were calling to her from his remote mountain hideaway.

Now she was seeing the almost mystical experience of the evening before in a more grounded way. Diego might not be still at the old monastery. But Rosa and Manuel would be able to tell her where she could find him; they would give her the address of his home near Jerez and his place of business.

And she knew that when she eventually ran him to earth her admission of love might well leave him cold; he might simply tell her he wasn't interested. That was something she would have to accept.

Even so, she was doing the right thing. There was a smooth, untroubled logic to it. Things left undone, important things, didn't bring a peaceful mind. Ben had shown her that.

Soon after his accident, when he'd thought he might not make it, he'd said he needed to see her. He'd wanted to make sure she was all right, to tell her to come back home if things weren't working out for her, that she'd be welcome, no hard feelings. He hadn't wanted to leave the assurances unsaid.

And life was notoriously precarious. If something

happened either to her or, heaven forbid, Diego, before she'd put the record straight there would be no peace, no closure.

Tears were wetting her face when she eventually switched off the ignition on the forecourt. Briefly closing her eyes, she gave herself a few moments to quieten her mind before mopping the dampness away with a tissue, exiting and stretching her cramped muscles. She took a deep breath and walked steadily over the sun-baked slabs towards the main door.

Her mouth ran dry and her heart banged savagely against her ribs. Would he refuse to let her cross the threshold? Refuse to listen to what she had to say? Had she come on a fool's errand?

Don't even think about it—don't accept defeat until it's inevitable. Think of something else, or don't think at all!

The late afternoon sun burned through the thin cotton of her blouse. But at this time of year the evenings in the mountains would be decidedly chilly. Had she packed a sweater? Did it matter?

'Señorita!' The great door swung open and Rosa's pretty face was wreathed in a beaming smile. Lisa gulped and did her best to return it.

'I heard the car. So it is you—you stay?'

Lisa tucked a heavy strand of hair behind her ear, took a steadying breath. 'I'm not sure.' And wasn't that the truth—she could be thrown out in two seconds flat. 'But I'd like to speak to the *señor*. If you'd tell him I'm here, please.'

'Come—' Rosa ushered her into the cool vastness

of the great hall. 'I fetch Manuel. He has the good English. I have not so good.'

Not a bad idea at that, Lisa thought as she lowered herself into a heavily carved chair beneath the tall window flanking the door, wishing the flutter of internal nerves wasn't making her feel quite so nauseous. There had been too many misunderstandings in the past; they could all do without any more. Though she'd have thought that a simple request to tell Diego she was here would have been easy enough to understand.

By the time Manuel put in an appearance Lisa was pacing the floor, mentally climbing walls, about to go in search of Diego herself because this waiting, this not knowing what her reception would be was killing her.

Twirling on her heels she faced him, nerves pattering. Soon now she would see her love—

'Rosa tells me you have come back from England to meet with the *señor*.' His swarthy features were sympathetic. 'But he is not here. He left very early this morning before it was light.'

'I see.' The tension drained out of her, quickly replaced by a dull sense of frustration. Nothing to get in a panic about, though. She had half-expected it, mentally prepared herself for this eventuality, hadn't she?

She'd missed him by a whisker.

'Then perhaps you could give me addresses of where I might find him?'

He seemed to consider her request for a long moment, then grinned. 'Perhaps I do better! Rosa is making coffee for you. She will bring it to small salon and I will make the phone calls. It is better to know for sure he is home—he might have gone anywhere in the world—his business affairs take him to many places.'

Sickening thought!

Impulsively, Lisa reached out to touch his arm as he began to leave her, her eyes unknowingly full of stark inky appeal, the hand that clutched his arm shaking just a little. 'I'd love coffee. It's been a long drive. But may I have it in the kitchen with Rosa?' She didn't want to be alone to agonise over the very real possibility that Diego was even now on his way to the other side of the world.

'Certainly.' His dark eyes were kind. 'Come with me. You drink coffee and I use the telephone.'

The main kitchen was cavernous with a vaulted stone and timber ceiling and a huge open fireplace. Nevertheless the atmosphere was surprisingly homelike, with hams, strings of onions and dried herbs hanging from the massive beams, the aroma of coffee drifting like a blessing.

Manuel said something to his wife in rapid Spanish as she turned from the huge gleaming range, a cafetière in one hand.

'Ciertamente!' Rosa smiled in response to whatever her husband had said, setting the coffee on an immense wooden table near a bowl of yellow roses, plucked, Lisa guessed, from the many blooms that perfumed the courtyard. 'All of us will drink! You will please to sit, *señorita*?'

Taking the chair indicated, Lisa sat and closed her

tired eyes for a moment, the quiet, comforting atmosphere helping her to wind down just a little. Rosa fetched three bowl-shaped coffee mugs and a plate of sticky almond pastries and Manuel consulted a list pinned up by the wall-mounted phone and began at last to dial.

Drinking the welcome coffee and queasily refusing the pastries, Lisa wished she could understand Manuel's side of the conversations that ensued as he dialled at least three separate numbers. Diego was obviously proving harder to track down than she had hoped.

A point punched home when he walked back to take his mug of coffee from the table, shrugging his shoulders fatalistically.

'I called the *señor's* office first. He has not been there. His sister hasn't seen him since she left here with her husband and his housekeeper gave us the only clue we have.' He spread his free hand as if to indicate the clue was sadly worthless. 'The *señor* phoned to his home at mid-morning to say to cancel the dinner he had arranged to give his parents next week. Is all. He didn't say where he was going, only that he had no idea when he would return.'

It was another perfect morning but Lisa couldn't begin to appreciate it. Something inside her had died. Diego could be anywhere in the world. True, she'd asked Manuel to ask Diego to get in touch with her when he saw him next. But she wasn't holding out much hope that he would bother to respond. He was getting on with his busy, successful life. He didn't need her in it.

Yesterday, the afternoon had been drawing to a close, the shadows lengthening on the mountains, when she'd thanked Rosa and Manuel for their help, hardly able to hide her misery, and made to leave.

But Manuel had firmly argued against her driving back to Seville, pointing out that she had already had a long journey from England, that it would soon be dark, and Rosa could quickly make the bed up in the room she'd had before. It would be no trouble, he'd insisted.

So she'd stayed the night, giving in because she had no energy left to fight for her own way—her need to get away from this beautiful place where she had been, so very briefly, happy and hopeful. Staying overnight had been sensible, she supposed, but she wished she hadn't slept late after the initial long restless hours.

Hurriedly, she stripped her bed and repacked the few overnight things she'd needed and carried the case down to the hired car.

She'd already said her goodbyes and thanks to Rosa and Manuel and while she'd been eating the very late breakfast the pretty housekeeper had insisted on making for her, Manuel had offered to try again to track Diego down for her.

He could telephone the *señor*'s parents; why hadn't he thought of that before? There was a slim hope. The *señor* didn't answer to them for what he was doing but they might know where he was. Though he doubted it. Hadn't the *señor*'s housekeeper had to give them his message? Which meant he hadn't spoken to them himself, didn't it? Nevertheless, for the *señorita*'s sake, he would try.

But the phone was dead. A problem with the line; it often happened, the Spaniard said with a shrug of resignation. So even the final slim hope of making contact with him was gone. There was nothing to keep her here.

Starting the engine, she said her silent farewells. There would be no closure and she'd just have to live with that. Get on with her life, just as he was doing.

Diego forced himself to slow down as the road twisted sharply, the wheels spinning on the loose surface. He wasn't suicidal; he was merely in a desperate hurry!

He vented a vehement string of oaths, his hard profile clenched. Everything was conspiring against him. He remembered what he'd told Lisa five years ago. He'd said his love had no ending and had meant it. Still did.

But finding her and proving it, demanding that she give him a chance to make her understand that she could find happiness as his wife—not Clayton's—was turning out to be a problem of nightmare proportions.

It had been mid-afternoon yesterday when he'd arrived at her flat. No answer. A phone call to her father had given him the information that she was staying with the Claytons in Holland Park, just until Ben was out of danger. The older man had sounded defensive, almost as if he were reluctant to let him know where his daughter was or what she was doing.

The taxi that had taken him to the Holland Park address had been frustratingly slow through the heavy traffic. Sophie, his rival's twin, had answered his summons, peering behind him. 'Where's Lise?'

'That's what I'd like to know.' Still sitting at Clayton's bedside, mopping his brow, feeding him grapes and kissing him better? The thought made him furious.

'She isn't with you, then?'

'Obviously not.' He had a hard time of it, hanging on to the very last thread of his rapidly dwindling patience. 'Why would she be?'

'Because she flew out to Spain this morning to see you. She said you had unfinished business. Look, she didn't put me in the picture, but she did say she didn't know when she'd be back. Ben's making good progress so I suppose she feels she doesn't need to be here now.' She widened the door aperture. 'Won't you come in?'

What the hell for? had been his initial, ill-mannered answer, happily unvoiced. He made himself smile. 'No. No, thank you.' And then, as if on an afterthought, 'Is Lisa's engagement to Ben still on?'

Sophie stared at him as if he'd been speaking double Dutch, then denied, 'No, of course not. I would have thought you, of all people, would have known that.'

Which had left him with a lot to think about. Just as he had come to London to find her, she had flown out to Spain to see him. Their planes had probably passed in mid-air, going in opposite directions! That surely had to mean she hadn't written him off as the uncaring boor he must have appeared during the final hours they'd spent together.

And her engagement to Clayton was still off. So why had she told Isabella she was soon to be married to the man whose ring she wore?

He must have taken his leave of Sophie but he couldn't remember having done so. He remembered walking further down the street, hailing a cab to take him back to the airport and using his mobile to phone Manuel to tell him to keep Lisa where she was until he got back.

The line was engaged. It was still engaged twenty minutes later. He tried again when he was dropped off at the airport and nearly exploded with frustrated fury.

The line was dead. The phone at the monastery was out. Finding him gone, no one knowing where he was, Lisa would have made tracks.

He had two options. Sit on the Claytons' doorstep until she decided to return. Or get back to Spain, hoping she'd still be there, waiting for him. Even if she'd left, which seemed more than likely, she might have told his staff where she was heading—directly home, or not.

There was too much adrenalin pumping round his veins to allow for inaction. He booked the last remaining seat on the early flight out to Seville then took himself off to the arrivals hall to wait for the late night flight in, hoping she might have been on it.

She wasn't.

And now he was wishing the last few miles away, undoubtedly looking like something the cat had dragged in, hoping against hope that she hadn't already left the monastery.

His thoughts grimly occupied, he had to stamp on the brakes to avoid a head-on collision with a Seat being driven the other way. As it was they were bumper to bumper. *Cristo!* Some people weren't fit to be behind the wheel; the driver had taken the tight bend at a maniac speed!

And there was no way he could pass; the road was too narrow. The other driver would have to back up, pronto. He was in a hurry!

His jawline set, shadowed with an overnight beard growth, he slid out of the car, took two stormy paces and his heart stopped.

Lisa!

His heart crashed on then melted as he watched her open the door at her side and slowly swing her long legs to the ground. She stood, lifting her face to him. She was pale, those beautiful eyes shadowed, her hair tumbling down in wayward tendrils. Her soft mouth quivered as their eyes meshed. He had never loved her more.

His driving aim to kiss that look of uncertainty from those haunted eyes, those trembling lips, had him landing one hand on the bonnet of his car and vaulting over the obstruction. Only one pace was necessary to bring him to his heart's desire. One forceful pace and he was holding her in his arms, fiercely pressed against his heart, groaning thickly as he felt her delicate body shake.

Then she slithered even closer into him, winding her arms around his neck, lifting her lovely face to his. There were tears in her eyes. His heart jerked. There must be no sadness. Not for her, not ever again. He would not allow it!

'Diego—'

'Hush,' he commanded thickly. 'No words. Just this—' He lowered his head to kiss her.

Lisa knew she was in heaven. Joy leapt through every vein and sinew and all the cells in her body were on fire as she kissed him back, her hunger matching his as she strainingly attempted to writhe closer even though that was not possible.

Their bodies were welded. She could feel the heated hardness of him through the barrier of their clothes. Lightning exploded inside her.

One of his hands was tangling in her hair. She could feel him shaking with the intensity of the passion that was claiming them both as reluctantly he dragged his mouth from hers and stated raggedly, 'You will marry me. You will forget Clayton, forget you ever knew him. If he weren't already lying injured on a hospital bed I would have beaten him to a pulp!'

He planted a kiss on her startled mouth, impressing his forceful decision. Lisa gurgled with laughter and kissed him back, only to find his dark head rearing away, a ferocious glitter in his dark eyes. 'This is no laughing matter. You are mine and I am a possessive man. I mean what I say. I propose to you and you giggle!' Violently insulted male pride bristled from every pore. 'But this time,' he uttered darkly, 'you do not leave my sight until I have my wedding ring on your finger. And not even then.'

'No problem. You won't be able to get rid of me,' Lisa assured him, a soft smile curling her mouth. 'And leave poor Ben out of it. I was engaged to him for a few hours. I have no intention of marrying him. There is no need to be jealous, and your proposal leaves a lot to be desired,' she added with teasing severity, safe now in the mind-blowing knowledge that the love of her life wasn't lost at all; he'd just been mislaid for a while.

His lean hands tightening on her shoulders, one black brow rose as he questioned, 'Then why did you flaunt his ring in front of me, tell Isabella that you would be marrying him soon?'

At least she had the grace to blush, Diego conceded, magnanimously deciding that he had already forgiven her for not knowing her own mind at that time. Hadn't she come back to Spain to find him and although she hadn't formally accepted his proposal—and how did it leave a lot to be desired?—she hadn't been able to hide the way she felt about him when he'd kissed her.

Her colour receding as she recalled just how dreadful she'd felt that last morning, her glance was direct as she offered contritely, 'It was stupid of me. But at the time it seemed the easiest way to shut her up. You were treating me as if I were a nasty smell and I was so miserable, so sure you wanted nothing more to do with me after the things I'd accused you of, I couldn't face explaining that I was only wearing the ring for safe-keeping. Your sister would just have asked more questions—'

'Isabella hasn't known how to keep silent since the

day she first learned to talk,' he acknowledged. 'Even so, you couldn't wait to leave me when you knew he'd been injured and when I asked if you loved him you said you did. You can't begin to imagine how that made me feel.'

'Oh, I can!' she whispered emotionally, lifting her hands to touch his lean and handsome face. 'When I thought you'd turned your back on me my whole world fell apart, my darling. And I do love Ben. But like a brother. Not as I love you.'

He pulled in a breath. His stunning eyes glittered as he commanded, 'Say that again. Say you love me!'

'Why else do you think I'm here? I knew I couldn't go through the rest of my life without telling you how deeply I love you.' Her voice wobbled. 'But you weren't here. Where were you?'

Completely consoled, Diego trailed loving kisses down the length of her throat. 'In London,' he murmured thickly. 'Looking for you. I, too, had to tell you that I loved you more than my life.' His lips encountered the top button of her cotton blouse. Slightly unsteady hands lifted to slip it out of its moorings, then stilled. With a supreme effort he controlled the fierce need to make love to his beautiful darling right here and now.

'We are blocking the road, my angel. We must go.' The lightest of kisses on her unbearably sensitised lips. 'Wait in my car. I will move the Seat.'

No sooner said than he was behind the wheel, reversing the little car in a cloud of dust. And within moments he was striding back to where she was frozen to the spot, immobilised by the utter magic of what was happening. Diego loved her! She was to be his wife! Welded to his side for the rest of their lives! How could anything in the world possibly be more wonderful?

All macho confidence, Diego opened the passenger door and gently eased her poleaxed body inside, strapping her in with cool efficiency before walking round to get behind the wheel, telling her, 'It is parked in a pull-in. And there it may stay,' with a calm disregard for the need to get it back to the hire firm at the airport. 'You, my most precious love, are going nowhere. And this time I keep you here with love. My bad behaviour is a thing of the past.' His hand on the ignition key, he turned to her, his eyes drenched with tenderness. 'For five years you haunted me. When I saw how I could take what I believed was my right to vengeance, I took it. Can you forgive me?'

'I can't blame you for thinking bad things about me,' Lisa confessed earnestly. 'Five years ago I behaved like a spoiled brat. I'd seen you with this fabulous woman. Twice. Once going into a jeweller's, and again in the hotel foyer. I thought you'd dumped me for her, that you hadn't meant it when you said you were in love with me. I—' her voice almost disintegrated '—I took my own childish form of revenge.'

'*Querida*—' His hands took hers, pressing kisses into her palms. 'That is all forgotten. But I need to hear you say you forgive me for my truly vile treatment once I had you to myself. I wanted you like crazy and I knew you weren't indifferent to me. So I decided to let you stew, wondering when you would have to fulfil your part of the hellish bargain. Increase the sexual tension until you begged me to make love to you. How can you love such a monster?'

'How can I stop?' she replied, sincerity spilling from her eyes. 'Besides, you gave me the option of leaving when it came right down to it, remember? So you can't be all bad!'

And with that assurance he gave her the slashing grin that had always had the power to turn her knees to water and started the engine.

It was growing dark, a soft amethyst light stealing over the mountains. Lisa, watching for the first faint stars from the terrace, wondered where Diego had got to.

She'd bathed and changed as he'd suggested, dressing with immense care in one of the beautiful dresses that she'd never expected to see again. A honey-coloured silk shift that made the most of her slender curves, her hair loose around her shoulders, her make-up as perfect as she could manage given that her fingers, all the cells in her body, were trembling with delicious anticipation.

'Come.' He was behind her, his hands lightly on her shoulders as he turned her to face him. She hadn't heard him approach. Her heart leapt.

'You are so beautiful,' he announced with betraying huskiness, beautiful himself in a formal white jacket over a pristine shirt and those narrow black trousers that made his sex-appeal positively killing.

Dreamily, she allowed herself to be led back

through the silent house. And only when he opened the door to his bedroom did her love-drenched eyes sparkle with delight.

The softly lit room was full of flowers—someone must have denuded the garden and the courtyard! There was champagne on ice and hauntingly sweet music coming from a hidden tape deck.

Wordlessly, he led her to the bedside where the satin covered pillows had been heaped to resemble a throne. He eased her down then with a flourish went down on one knee and took her hand.

A dark flush emphasising his slashing cheekbones, his voice deep with emotion, he asked, 'Lisa, will you marry me if I ask, leaving nothing to be desired?'

Her throat closed up. Speechless at first, her heart feeling as though it had no option but to burst, she lifted the hand that was gripping hers so tightly and kissed the back of each of those strong lean fingers with fevered intensity until she was able to whisper, 'Yes! Oh, yes, my darling!'

Several breathless minutes later, after the throne-like position of the heaped pillows had been thoroughly disturbed, Diego eased himself away from her and slipped a ring on her finger. The beautiful sapphire gleamed in the soft light. 'This is the ring I chose for you five years ago. It is now where it belongs.'

Her eyes brimmed with delirious tears and Diego took his time over kissing them away, only stopping when her fingers clamped around his wrist and she stated happily, 'You didn't throw it away.'

'Throw what away, my dearest angel?'

'The watch.' She'd seen the glint of gold.

For a moment he looked discomfited. Then he grinned, kissed her with swift passion and confessed, 'I have always worn it. Only when I got to London on my mission of vengeance did I replace it with some cheap horror bought from the airport duty free shop. If you'd seen it you would have known that you had been in my heart, had never left it. At the time giving you that knowledge was not on my agenda.'

'I see.' Her eyes sultry, Lisa trailed kisses down from his temples to his sensual mouth. 'So what is on your agenda now, I wonder.'

His mouth smiled beneath hers as his body pinned her back against the tumbled pillows. 'I'll give you three guesses, my dearest darling.'